This Means War!

This Means War!

ELLEN WITTLINGER

SCHOLASTIC INC.
New York Toronto London Auckland
Sydney Mexico City New Delhi Hong Kong

ISBN 978-0-545-34353-4

Copyright © 2010 by Ellen Wittlinger.
All rights reserved. Published by Scholastic Inc., 557 Broadway, New York, NY 10012, by arrangement with Simon & Schuster Books for Young Readers, an imprint of Simon & Schuster Children's Publishing Division. SCHOLASTIC and associated logos are trademarks and/or registered trademarks of Scholastic Inc.

12 11 10 9 8 7 6 5 4 3 2 1   11 12 13 14 15 16/0

Printed in the U.S.A.   40

First Scholastic printing, April 2011

Book design by Lucy Ruth Cummins
The text for this book is set in Garamond.

For my nephews:
Chris, Martin, David, Evan, and Jeffrey

Acknowledgments

Grateful thanks to my editor, David Gale; my agent, Ginger Knowlton; and my critique group—Nancy Werlin, Pat Lowry Collins, Liza Ketchum, and Lisa Papademetriou—for their help and advice on the manuscript.

This Means War!

chapter one

Juliet had hardly spoken to Lowell in weeks, or maybe he was the one who hadn't spoken to her. Whichever way it was, she didn't like it. So on Friday afternoon, even though she could see that Lowell was with his new friends, Mike and Tommy Lambert, Juliet hitched up her self-confidence like droopy kneesocks and crossed the alley to his yard.

Lowell and Tommy were sitting on the concrete under the carport, tightening, or maybe loosening, the back wheels of a go-kart that had showed up at Lowell's house just that week. Mike was sitting on a rusty lawn chair, a stack of comic books next to him, flipping through a *Mad* magazine.

"Hey, what are you guys doing?" Juliet barked out her question nervously, and it hung in the air for all of them to behold, like underwear on a clothesline.

"What does it look like we're doing?" Tommy said, without taking his eyes from the wheel. He was gritting his teeth as though screwing or unscrewing a bolt were an almost impossible task.

Juliet stared hard at Lowell until he looked back at her, a twitchy smile—here, then gone—the only sign that he recognized her. She pulled at the ends of her tight curls as if she could stretch them out longer than the tips of her ears. How could her best friend act like this?

Juliet and Lowell had been inseparable ever since his parents moved in across the alley six years before. They'd gone through school together since kindergarten, played a million games of Clue on his back porch, and gotten into trouble for tracking tar into her house on their bare feet. They'd spent whole summers filling water balloons and throwing them, first at cars and then at each other, and they'd ridden their bikes over every inch of Wisdom Hill, Illinois. Until suddenly, this fall, for some unfathomable reason, everything changed.

"When did you get a go-kart?" Juliet asked Lowell, trying another tactic. "I didn't even know you liked go-karts."

"I like them!" he said, glaring at her. "You don't know everything."

"It's ours," Mike said, throwing down the *Mad* and picking up an old issue of *Superman*, which Juliet figured was Lowell's, since he collected them.

"Why is it over here, then?" Juliet said. She wasn't happy with the way her voice sounded—it reminded her of her mother asking, "What are your shoes doing in the middle of the living room floor?" instead of just telling her to take them upstairs.

"There's no good place to work on it at our new house," Mike said. "We don't have a garage or a carport."

"We had a great garage in Omaha," Tommy said. "I liked that house better than the one here."

"Yeah," Mike agreed, "but I liked living in Virginia best of all."

Just as Juliet had suspected, the Lambert twins were Air Force brats, like so many of the new kids at school. Everything that was going wrong this year had to do with Lathrop Air Field, which lay on the outskirts of Wisdom Hill. Even the fact that there were two fifth-grade classes this fall instead of one was because they lived so close to the Field. Juliet's mother had said Lathrop was gearing up for the possibility of war, which was why more airmen and their families were moving to the area. Lathrop was one of the biggest air bases in the country, but living a few miles away from squadrons of bombers did not please Juliet.

After all, it was because of Lathrop Air Field that Lowell had been put into a fifth-grade class with a new teacher, Miss Abshire, who was young and pretty, while Juliet had been stuck without her best friend in crazy old Mrs. Funkhauser's class. And it was because of Lathrop Air Field that Lowell had met Mike and Tommy, who were also in Miss Abshire's class. And it was because of Lathrop Air

Field that there were two lunch periods now, and Juliet was in the first one and Lowell was in the second one. And it was because of Lathrop Air Field that she had nobody to trade sandwiches with anymore or chase around the baseball diamond at recess or laugh with about Mrs. Funkhauser's big mop of terrible hair. It was because of Lathrop Air Field that Juliet was, for the first time in her life, lonely.

Juliet realized she'd been staring at the cover of the *Superman* comic Mike was holding in front of his face. It was one of Lowell's favorite issues from last year—1961—when he'd begun collecting them in earnest. The Man of Steel was catching bombs in his hands and throwing them back at the bad guys. *If only the United States had a hero like that on their side,* she thought, *they wouldn't need so many Air Force bases.*

Mike caught her looking at the comic book. "We're kind of busy," he said. "You should probably go home."

"You're not busy," she said. "You're reading *Superman.*"

"Well, *we're* busy," Tommy said. "And we don't need any girls around getting in our way."

"I could help you," Juliet offered. "I make model cars sometimes, don't I, Lowell? Remember that Model T Ford we made last year?"

Lowell pressed his lips together and pulled at the back wheel of the go-kart with all his strength, but Juliet still couldn't tell if he was making sure it was on tight or trying to take it off.

"Remember?" she asked again.

"No," he said under his breath, then peered up at her, the lie making his freckles darken on his pale face.

"You do too remember!" she said, anger pushing up into her throat from the sore spot in her chest where she'd tried to keep it hidden. "You had it in your room on the windowsill for six months, and now I have it in my room!"

"So what?" Mike said, throwing down the comic. "Just because you can make a model car doesn't mean you can work on a go-kart. This is stuff that boys do, not girls."

"Says who? You think you're so smart just because your dad is at Lathrop. Big deal."

"Yeah, it is a big deal," Mike said. "Have you ever even *been* to the base?"

"Of course I have. Everybody round here's been there. I don't see what's so special about it. It's only got about six streets, and it's out in the middle of a cornfield."

In fact Juliet had only been to Lathrop once. Normally, civilians weren't allowed on base, but a few years back her family had gone there to see an air show put on by the Blue Angels, a precision flying team who kept their airplanes in tight formation as they soared and dove and turned somersaults in the sky. They were terribly loud as they came in

this means war! · 5

low over the crowd, and Juliet had been so scared she'd screamed bloody murder.

They'd had to leave before the show was over, but she remembered what the place looked like: big brick buildings surrounded by long barracks, all of them behind tall barbed-wire fences. The whole place had looked temporary to her, as if it had been set down out there in the middle of nowhere by a big, invisible hand, or maybe a tornado. She had the feeling the buildings might one day decide to up and move to some other patch of flat, dry land, and nobody would know they'd ever been there.

Mike snorted. "You don't know anything about it. Without air bases like Lathrop, the Communists would take over our country!"

Juliet was pretty sure Communists were Russians, but she didn't really know much about them. Still, she planted her feet on the concrete, perfectly willing to argue with Mike as long as it meant she could stick around for a while. If only Lowell's unhappy gaze hadn't settled on her face.

"You should go home," he said. "We're busy. We don't want any girls around."

Juliet felt her anger turn liquid and gather behind her eyes. How could Lowell be so mean to her for no reason at all? She would *never* treat him this way. He was her best friend in the world! Without another word she turned and walked back to her own side of the alley.

As she left, she heard Tommy start a knock-knock joke. The three of them were making boy-noise, just like they did at school—that kind of *here-I-am-look-at-me* boisterous squawking that made adults frown and other kids notice. When Lowell had been Juliet's friend, he'd been the quieter of the two of them and the one less likely to steer them into mischief, but things had changed. Now he was a big show-off, just like his Air Force–brat friends. Juliet couldn't hear the punch line of Tommy's joke, but she heard the boys laughing, and she imagined they were laughing at her.

chapter two

Lately, Juliet had been doing quite a bit of praying, at least for someone whose family only went to church on Christmas and Easter. The year before, after her grandpa passed away, Juliet had started praying not to die. She knew it was a lot to ask, so she asked it only for herself and for her family. She would be willing to lose everyone else if only the four of them could live forever, or at least for a very long time.

But if one of us has to die, Juliet thought, *we could sacrifice Caroline.*

And, really, she felt pretty proud of herself for even including her older sister in the original request, since Caroline usually treated *her* like a carrier of the black plague. For example, every time Caroline's friend Mimi came over lately, they kicked Juliet out of her own room, which was only 50 percent Caroline's.

Which is what Juliet told her Saturday morning. "This room is only fifty percent yours, Caroline, so don't boss me around. All you're going to do is listen to records anyway. And practice doing the Twist." Juliet swung her rear end back and forth in an exaggerated imitation of the latest dance craze.

"Jules, can't you go downstairs for a while?" Caroline begged. "We need some privacy."

"Yeah, get lost," Mimi added. Mimi only had brothers, so she didn't have to share a room with anybody and thought it was a horrible injustice that Caroline did.

"I need some privacy too!" Juliet said.

Caroline rolled her eyes. "Ten-year-olds don't need privacy. Besides, all you're doing is sitting on your bed staring out the window."

"I'm thinking," Juliet said.

Mimi frowned. "Ten-year-olds can't think. They can barely *read*."

"Maybe *you* could barely read at ten, but I've been reading and thinking for years already." Juliet couldn't imagine why Caroline was best friends with such an annoying person. Maybe there was something wrong with their whole family that made them choose lousy best friends.

"Why don't you go over to Lowell's?" Caroline suggested.

"I don't want to."

"Why not? You could take a bike ride together."

"Maybe they had a spat," Mimi said. "Did you have a fight with your little boyfriend?"

Juliet glared at Mimi. "He's not my boyfriend. Why are you so dumb?"

Mimi sneered and chuckled in a way that made Juliet want to bite her. "Just wait," Mimi said. "In another year or two you'll have a big old crush on Lowell."

"I will not!" Juliet scooted off her bed and slipped into her old penny loafers. Who would even want to stay in the room with girls who were so stupid? "I'm going, but not because you told me to. Because I can't stand to listen to you talk about boyfriends and crushes. It makes me want to puke."

She slammed the door behind her and clomped down the steep stairway, but she could still hear Caroline and Mimi cracking up, as if she'd just said something hilarious.

There was never any privacy downstairs. The first floor of their house had living quarters only in the back; in the front was her parents' store, Klostermeyer's Market, which hosted a steady stream of neighborhood customers, many of whom had been shopping there so long they felt they were members of the family and would poke their heads through the screen door that divided front from back and yell in their greetings. Or they'd smell whatever her mother had run back to stick in the oven, and they'd call through the open window between the store and the kitchen, "Ethel, are you making a pot roast for dinner?"

Even her mother sometimes got peeved at their nosiness. Actually, these days her mother got peeved at almost everything, which was another reason Juliet would just as soon not do her thinking downstairs. If Ethel Klostermeyer caught you doing nothing—which is what thinking looked like—she'd find a way for you to "make yourself useful," which meant some odious chore like ironing bedsheets or dusting the useless collection of cups and saucers that sat on a knickknack shelf in the dining room. Juliet's mother seldom sat still for more than five minutes at a time, and she didn't see why anyone else needed to either.

Juliet took her favorite cup out of the dish drainer and poured herself some ice water from the refrigerator. The cup, which had been her grandfather's, had a picture of a racehorse on the side. He'd gotten it at the Cahokia racetrack the one time he'd gone, and he wouldn't let anyone but Juliet use it. After he died, her grandma gave her the cup to remember him by, not that she could ever forget him anyway.

Out of everybody in her whole family, her grandpa was the one who had always had time for her. Everybody had said he spoiled her, but Juliet had never felt spoiled, only loved. She should have prayed that *he'd* never die, but she hadn't thought of it until it was too late. She didn't intend to make that mistake again. Of course, there was no use including her grandmother in her prayers, because Grandma herself was praying to "join Poppa in heaven." Juliet figured it would confuse God if they were asking for different things.

Peering out the living room window she could see that

there was nobody outside at Lowell's house, which was good. She could go out without having to see him and pretend she didn't. It was a warm, sunny day for October—she might as well take advantage of it and ride her bike. Since Saturdays were always busy in the store, chances were good that her mother wouldn't have time to stop and grill her about where she was going.

She stepped through the screen door and closed it quietly behind her. Her father was grinding hamburger meat for Mrs. Schneider, who was very picky and wouldn't buy anything that she hadn't watched go into the grinder herself; her mother was ringing up a big order for the Mattesons. Juliet stopped briefly at the candy case and reached a hand in to grab two Zero bars and a few pieces of black licorice.

"Is that Juliet?" Mrs. Matteson sang out. "My goodness, I haven't seen you in ages. You've gotten so tall!"

Juliet smiled and quickly stuck the candy bars in her jacket pocket. When her mother turned around, she saw only the licorice strips waving in her daughter's hand.

"Are you eating candy already? It's eleven o'clock in the morning."

"I'm just taking it with me," Juliet said. "I'm going for a bike ride."

"Don't cross the highway. You going with Lowell?"

Juliet shrugged. "I don't know."

Ethel's fingers danced over the tops of the tin cans as

her eyes darted back and forth between the register and the countertop. "Go ask him. I don't like you to ride alone."

Juliet sighed. "What difference does it make? I'm just as safe alone as I am with Lowell. He's not Superman, you know."

Ethel frowned at the canned goods. "Now I've lost my place. Did I ring in those cream corns? Juliet distracted me."

While her mother was busy comparing the register tape to the groceries, Juliet took the opportunity to sneak out the door into the garage and get her bike. She couldn't believe her mother hadn't even noticed that Lowell wasn't her friend anymore—he hadn't come over in weeks. But all her mother had time for these days was worrying about how to keep their customers from shopping at the big new supermarkets that had started to open up in town. No time for Juliet's little problems.

She wheeled her bike out of the garage. It had once been Caroline's bicycle, but Caroline wouldn't be caught dead riding it now. She and Mimi spent hours trying to figure out how to get boys with driver's licenses to take them places, although so far they hadn't had much luck. Juliet got on the bike and rolled out of her driveway and down the alley that ran between her house and Lowell's. She tried not to look over into his yard, but her head wouldn't obey her brain. Lowell's mom was out in their garden, pulling the last of the green beans from the vines. She waved.

"Hey, Juliet, we haven't seen much of you lately," she

called over. Lowell's mom looked just like him, small and blond, with big front teeth and a bigger smile.

Juliet waved back at Mrs. McManus. "Yeah, I guess I've been . . . busy." What she wanted to say was, *Don't you know that your son is being a jerk to me?* But instead she just smiled and pedaled on down the alley.

It had been a bad fall all around. Not only had Juliet lost her best friend, but the St. Louis Cardinals hadn't even come near to winning the National League pennant, which always put her father in a rotten mood. Last night at dinner he couldn't stop complaining about the president. "The world's going to hell in a handbasket, and all that Kennedy can talk about is putting a man on the moon. What good is a man on the moon going to do me? Or any normal person?"

"Don't be such a pessimist, Don," Ethel told him.

"I'm being realistic," he told her. "It's been a terrible year with all this talk about another war. Spy planes. Bombs. It makes people jumpy."

Juliet had gotten a funny taste in her mouth and couldn't finish her macaroni and cheese. She hated it when people talked about war. She knew that lots of people died in wars: Her father's brother, who would have been her uncle Peter, died in World War II, but they didn't talk about him a lot because it upset her dad so much. And the word "bomb" made Juliet feel lightheaded, like she might pass out. A bomb, she knew, didn't just kill soldiers; it killed anybody who was near it. And she didn't like hearing her father say that grown-ups were nervous too—that meant she wasn't just imagining how bad it could be.

"Every time the Cards lose, my business goes downhill, the winter's freezing, and another supermarket opens up in town."

"Oh, for Pete's sake, Don, the Cardinals are not in charge of the weather," Ethel said. "And supermarkets are going to open up no matter who wins the pennant. We're lucky we live in such a small town that it's taken a long time for them to get here. We just have to figure out a way to compete."

Don just shook his head. "I'm getting too old for it," he said.

"Fifty is not old," Ethel said.

"How would you know? You're not even forty yet."

It was an old argument between them: her father's age, her mother's youth. Juliet didn't like to think of her father being old and wished he wouldn't dwell on it so much. It made her worry about how much longer he'd be around. And then she'd pray some more. *Dear God, please don't let Dad die for a long, long time. Or Mom, either. Or me. I guess Caroline could stay on earth a while longer too. And please don't let a war start. In case you don't know, there are really bad bombs now which can kill thousands of people at one time. Which doesn't seem like the kind of thing you'd approve of. So keep an eye on that, okay?*

Mrs. Shepard's dog, Boneguard, rushed to the fence as Juliet pedaled by. Most kids in the neighborhood were scared of him; he was an enormous animal who bared his teeth when anybody came near the house and looked like he'd be happy to snack on your fingers before devouring your face. But Juliet was a dog lover without a dog—Caroline had allergies—so Mrs. Shepard had let her come over and play with Boneguard when he was a puppy, and the dog seemed to remember her. Although now that he'd grown to be the size of a small piano, she was more hesitant to test his memory.

"Hey, Boney," she yelled, and the dog stopped barking. His lip was still curled back, though, and his teeth were larger than the Big Bad Wolf's, so Juliet rode on. As she passed the Schlossers' house, which had a FOR SALE sign on the lawn, and old Cotton Mondale's big backyard full of dried-up cornstalks and sunflowers, she promised herself that she was going to make some new friends. Or at least one new friend. One good one was all you really needed. Somebody she could ride bikes with and invite to her room when Caroline and Mimi weren't hogging it. Somebody she could talk to the way she used to be able to talk to Lowell.

It wouldn't be easy to find that kind of friend, though. The two girls in her class who she'd been most friendly with over the years, Annette Hendricks and Linda Wheeler, ate lunch with her in the cafeteria now, but she mostly just sat between them and let their arguments bounce off her.

Annette would say something like, "Billy Holtz is adorable, don't you think? He cut the grass for my parents all summer and I got to watch him from my window."

"Billy *Holtz*?" Linda would say, incredulous. "He's in high school!"

"So what? I can look at him, can't I?"

"What if he saw you looking? I would *die*! Wouldn't you just *die*, Juliet?"

Juliet would shrug, and the conversation would go on without her. She didn't even know who Billy Holtz was, and she didn't care if he was adorable or not, and she certainly wouldn't die just because somebody saw her *looking* at them. Annette and Linda sounded too much like Caroline and Mimi for Juliet's taste. So she would just pick the crusts off her sandwich and suck her milk container dry and wish she had somebody else to talk to.

When she came to the end of the alley, Juliet turned right onto Boxfield Road, figuring to head out into the countryside and look at the pumpkins that were still left in the fields. She swung her bike out of the alley, around an enormous rose of Sharon bush, and onto the sidewalk, where, unexpectedly, there was another bicycle, stopped dead.

"Whoa!" Juliet cried as she clipped the other bike, steered hers onto the lawn, and then hopped off before it fell over. "Jeez, I didn't see you there!"

"Sorry," the other girl said. She had golden-orange hair

that puffed out from her head like dandelion fuzz. "I guess I was daydreaming. Are you okay?"

"Yeah, fine," Juliet said, picking up her bike. "Are you?"

The girl nodded. "I never get hurt."

"You should pull your bike off onto the lawn if you aren't riding it. Kids come flying up the alley and around that corner all the time."

"Okay," the girl said, and walked her bike off the path. "Do you live around here?"

Juliet pointed. "Up on Abbott Street. Where do you live?"

"Right there," the girl said, pointing to the small white house with the blue front door that they were standing in front of. "We just moved here from Arizona. We got here yesterday, and our furniture came today."

"You did? Wow, that's . . . neat." Juliet smiled a little nervously and tried not to stare at the girl, but it was hard not to. She was kind of strange-looking, tall and skinny with a dark tan and that weird hair. Juliet herself had Toni Home Permanent curls—boring little brown circles, not wild, flying fluff like this girl's.

"Hey, how come they call this place Wisdom Hill?" the girl asked. "I haven't seen anything that looks like a hill since we came through southern Missouri. It's pancake flat around here."

Juliet nodded. "I know. I guess there's this little hill on a farm on the west end of town where these people named

Wisdom used to live. I've never seen it, though."

"So Wisdom Hill isn't hilly." The girl cocked her head the way dogs sometimes do. "It's probably not wise, either."

Juliet laughed. "You're right—it isn't. Funny, I never really thought about the name of the town before. It's just where I live."

The girl sighed. "Well, I guess now it's where I live too." She didn't sound all that happy about it.

Slowly, it began to dawn on Juliet that here was a kid who seemed to be about her own age who lived just down the street from her. Maybe this was her new friend! Lowell could spend the rest of his life screwing wheels off and on that dumb go-kart with those stupid Lambert twins—she wouldn't need him anymore.

"What's your name?" Juliet asked the girl with the dandelion hair.

"Patricia Marie Osgood. But everybody calls me Patsy, except my mother. What's yours?"

"Juliet Klostermeyer. I don't have a middle name, because my mother didn't want to take a chance that people would call me anything except Juliet. She loves that name," Juliet said, rolling her eyes.

Patsy's eyes widened. "Klostermeyer! That's the name of the grocery store up the street."

Juliet nodded. "My parents own it. We live behind it and upstairs."

"That's boss! I was in there this morning with my mom. There's a lot of candy in your store. Do you get to have it whenever you want?"

Juliet put her hand in her pocket and smiled as she withdrew the slightly smushed Zero bars. The licorice strips hadn't lasted the length of the alley.

"You are so lucky!" Patsy said. "I'd give anything to live at a grocery store! Can you walk into the store and get Fudgsicles and Twinkies and stuff like that too?"

Juliet shrugged. "Only if I sneak them. My mom thinks everything that tastes good ruins your appetite."

Patsy nodded. "My mom's like that too."

Juliet looked at her two candy bars and made a spur of the moment decision. "You can have one if you want. I can always get more."

"Really?" Patsy took the Zero bar that Juliet held out to her. "Thanks."

They stripped away the candy wrappers and bit into the gooey sweetness in companionable silence. Smacking her lips, Patsy downed hers in two bites.

chapter three

Juliet followed Patsy into the white house with the blue door. Like most of the homes at this end of Wisdom Hill, the house was small but well kept up. There were two chairs and a sofa in the living room, Juliet noticed, but so many boxes were piled around and on top of them you couldn't have sat on the furniture if you'd wanted to.

Patsy's mother was standing at the kitchen counter, unwrapping newspaper from a boxful of dishes. She was wearing a loose dress, and her hair, which was almost as frizzy as Patsy's, was held out of her face with a blue bandana.

"Patricia Marie, you know you could be of some help to me . . . ," she started to say, but then looked up and saw Juliet standing behind her daughter. "Oh, goodness, I didn't realize . . ." She put her hand to her head as if to fix her hair. "Hello, there."

"Hi," Juliet said.

"This is Juliet," Patsy explained. "She lives up at the grocery store—Klostermeyer's. And she wants me to ride bikes with her around the neighborhood. Okay?"

Mrs. Osgood pulled out a kitchen chair and sank into it, obviously glad of an excuse to sit down for a minute.

"Well, Juliet, very nice to meet you." She stuck out her hand and Juliet shook it, wondering if she'd ever shaken hands with a grown-up before; they usually didn't bother to do it with kids.

"Nice to meet you, too," Juliet said.

"How old are you, Juliet?" Mrs. Osgood asked.

"I'm ten."

"So am I!" Patsy said. "Do you go to the Jefferson School?"

"Yeah! Are you in fifth grade?"

"Yeah! My teacher has a funny name . . ."

"Mrs. Funkhauser! She's my teacher!" Juliet said. "We're in the same class!" Both girls jumped up and down a little.

"Have you lived here a long time, Juliet?" Mrs. Osgood wanted to know.

"Forever. My mom and dad grew up about a mile down the road. They lived across the street from each other. My dad was just home from the war, and staying with his parents while he figured out what to do next, and he was twelve years older than my mom, and they . . . they met each other." Suddenly, Juliet thought maybe this was what her mother called "running off at the mouth" and "telling everything you know," which was not appropriate to do with people you'd just met.

But Mrs. Osgood had such a nice smile Juliet thought it would be easy to feel like you'd known her a long time.

"Well, I'm glad Patricia Marie has met someone who can help her get adjusted to things here," Mrs. Osgood said. "We've had to move pretty often over the years, and she doesn't enjoy it."

Patsy looked down at her tennis shoes. "Sometimes I don't mind so much, but we were in Tucson for more than two years, and I got to know a lot of kids. I really liked living there. I coulda stayed there forever."

"I know, sweetheart. I liked it there too, but the Air Force makes those decisions for us." Patsy's mother bent down to pick up some newspaper that had fallen to the floor and stuffed it in a metal trash can.

"Is your dad a pilot?" Juliet asked. "I heard they were bringing lots more pilots to Lathrop Air Field."

"No," Patsy said, frowning a little. "He's a mechanic. If it was me, though, I'd be a pilot!"

A deep voice boomed from the garage, which opened off the kitchen. "Just how long do you think those B-52s would stay up in the air if there weren't any mechanics to fix them when they broke? Being a mechanic is just as important a job as sitting on your rear end in the cockpit!"

Patsy nodded. "I know, Dad. And you're the best mechanic there is."

Patsy's mom picked another newspaper-wrapped plate

from the box. "If you girls are going to take a bike ride, do it now. Dad's about to go to the hardware store with David, but when they get back, I'd like you to entertain your brother so we can get some work done around here."

Patsy's face darkened. "David's going with Dad? Dad, you said I could go with you!"

"You can come too if you want."

"You just said you wanted to ride bikes with Juliet," Patsy's mother reminded her.

"I do, but . . . David always gets to go places with Dad." She kicked her tennis shoe into the cabinet under the sink.

Patsy's reaction surprised Juliet. She couldn't remember the last time she'd gone anywhere or done anything with her dad. Nor did she particularly want to. Where would they go? To the slaughterhouse? No, thanks.

A tall, heavyset man stepped into the kitchen. He had on greasy overalls and shoes with round, fat toes. "Now, Patsy, don't be that way. David's a boy—he's interested in the same kinds of things I'm interested in, that's all." He nodded hello to Juliet, and she smiled back.

A towheaded boy with a finger stuck in his nose scooted in behind Patsy's father and stuck out his tongue. "Yeah, me and Dad is the same, Patsy."

Juliet thought David was a cute little kid, but Patsy obviously felt differently.

"David's five years old!" she shouted. "He doesn't care

about the hardware store! I'm the one who likes looking at all the different kinds of nails and stuff!"

"You can go with me next time," her dad said, winking at Juliet as if he'd just shared a secret with her.

"Just me and not David?"

"Okay. Next time, just you."

"No fair! No fair!" David screamed.

"You two drive me nuts," Patsy's mom said, scooting David back out into the garage. "Patsy, go take your bike ride now. Be back in an hour or so."

"Let's go," Juliet said. "So we have enough time." Patsy followed her outside, letting the screen door bang behind them.

"Do you have a brother?" she asked Juliet.

"No. I have an older sister, though. She bugs the heck out of me sometimes."

Patsy frowned. "There's nothing worse than a younger brother. David is such a brat, but my Dad acts like he's perfect. Just because he's a boy!"

They mounted their bikes, and Juliet took the lead, riding farther down Boxfield Road until they came to Grove Street. "Let's go up here; I'll show you where my grandma and grandpa used to live," Juliet said. They pedaled around the corner and halfway down the block before Juliet slowed down and jumped off her bicycle.

"There. In that little green house. They lived there until

Grandpa died last year." Even now, more than a year later, saying it out loud made Juliet's voice thicken and her heart thump. "My grandma is in a nursing home now, so we sold the house to these people who just got married. There's a great climbing tree in the backyard. You can see it if you look through there," Juliet said, pointing.

"That's a boss tree," Patsy agreed. "You could go way out on some of those branches."

"I have."

"I'm a boss tree climber," Patsy said. "I can climb *anything*."

Juliet was a very good tree climber too, but she didn't like bragging, so she changed the subject. "How many grandparents do you have?"

"I still got three. How about you?"

"Just one now. My dad's parents died before I was born. And Mom's dad died last year." Remembering the day her grandpa died made Juliet's stomach feel hollowed out. She'd been down to visit her grandparents that Saturday morning with her mother, and Grandpa had taken her into the backyard to show her the new bird feeder he'd just finished making. After that they'd picked milkweed pods and cracked them open, getting the sticky milk on their fingers and blowing the white feathers all around the yard.

Around dinnertime Grandma had called up, crying. It was a heart attack. He was dead before the ambulance arrived. Juliet still couldn't believe that a person she'd loved so much could be gone so quickly and forever.

"Are there many kids around here?" Patsy asked.

"Not so many on this street. But in *that* house . . ." Juliet had her finger in the air when the door to the house she was pointing to opened, and a tallish boy with a long neck and a flat-top haircut swaggered out onto the porch and looked straight at them. He had a pack of cigarettes rolled into the sleeve of his T-shirt.

"Whatcha lookin' at, moron?" he yelled at Juliet.

"Darn it!" Juliet said, turning to Patsy with a panicky look in her eyes. "Ride fast until we get by him. I'll tell you why later."

But Patsy stood her ground. "It's a free country!" she yelled back at the kid. "We can ride our bikes here if we want to!"

"You're on my property, and I don't like it," the boy said as he came down the front steps. He picked up a tree branch that had fallen on the lawn and hit it against his leg so it made a smacking sound.

Juliet had already pedaled past the boy's house, but now she stopped and looked back. "Come on, Patsy. He's a jerk," she called.

But Patsy wasn't ready to run. "You don't own the sidewalk, nosebleed. You can't tell me what to do."

"Oh, can't I?" The boy swung the stick so it arced toward

Patsy's head. It would have hit her if she hadn't ducked aside.

"Missed me!" Patsy called happily as she hopped on her bike and rolled past the boy and on down the sidewalk. She was still laughing when she and Juliet got to the end of the street.

"I can't believe you did that!" Juliet said as they stopped to reconnoiter. "Nobody talks back to him."

"Why not? Who is he? I don't like him," Patsy said.

"Nobody likes him," Juliet said. "He's mean as a poked rattlesnake. His name is Bruce Wagner, and he's in the sixth grade at Jefferson, but he oughta be in seventh already. They held him back because he skips school so much. His parents are divorced, and his mother can't make him behave. He used to throw rocks at me and Lowell when we rode our bikes to school. He'd hide behind an old shed and jump out and scare us."

"Who's Lowell?"

Oh, Lord, there was an awful lot Patsy didn't know about the neighborhood. Juliet wondered if an hour was going to be enough time to tell her everything.

"Lowell used to be my best friend. He lives in that yellow house down there," Juliet said, pointing again.

"He wasn't your boyfriend, was he?" Patsy asked.

"No! I don't have boyfriends. He was just my friend."

"But he's not anymore?"

Juliet shook her head. "This year he got to be friends

with these two new boys, Mike and Tommy, and they act like I'm poisonous or something. They don't want me around because I'm a girl."

"Boys are idiots," Patsy said, frowning down the street toward Lowell's house.

"I don't get it. I was a girl last year and the year before that and the year before that, too. And Lowell didn't seem to mind then. How come all of a sudden he doesn't like girls anymore?"

Patsy shrugged. "Who knows? But at least now *you* got a new friend too."

Juliet was surprised. Were they really friends already? Had Patsy decided she liked her in just these few blocks? Maybe Air Force kids always made friends fast; Juliet guessed you'd have to if you moved all the time.

"How many places have you lived?" Juliet asked.

Patsy threw her head back to think. "Well, Tucson, Arizona, for almost two and half years—that was my favorite place—and before that San Antonio, Texas, but only one year there, and before that we were in California . . ."

"Really? I want to go to California sometime! Did you ever see any movie stars?"

Patsy shook her head. "No. We lived in the middle of nowhere. Nothin' around but the Mojave Desert."

Juliet thought the Mojave Desert sounded exciting too. She'd certainly never seen a desert.

"And before that I think was Spokane, Washington, and before that someplace in Virginia, but I don't really remember those places very well. I was pretty little."

"I think you're really lucky," Juliet said. "I've never been farther than St. Louis, Missouri. Well, we spent a week in the Ozarks last summer, but that's not very far away. And all there is to do there is fish and drink beer. I mean, I didn't drink beer, but my parents sure did. I'd rather go to all the places you've been!"

Patsy laughed the big laugh Juliet was already beginning to appreciate; it came from deep inside her and wrapped around you so you felt like laughing too. "You wouldn't think so if you had to move all the time. Just when I get to really liking someplace, I have to pack up and go somewhere else."

"How long do you think you'll get to stay here?"

She shrugged. "Who knows? At least a year, though. Dad says a lot of people are being sent to Lathrop now in case there's a war with Russia. Lathrop is one of the bases that'll be activated first."

War. Why did it have to sneak into every darn conversation these days? Just the mention of it brought that scared, sick feeling back to Juliet's stomach. The duck-and-cover drills at school were bad enough, but her mother listened to the television news most nights now too, and all they talked about were bombs and missiles. How were you supposed to laugh at *The Jetsons* after that? People talked about war way too much, especially considering that there didn't seem to be much you could actually *do* about it. Except crouch down under your desk and pray to whoever you thought might be listening.

To put the subject behind them Juliet said, "Are you hungry? We could go to my house and get something to eat."

"Yeah! Could we get Fudgsicles?"

"Maybe. My mom might want to make us eat sandwiches first, though."

"Bologna sandwiches? You got bologna?"

"I live in a store and my dad is a butcher. We have lunch meats you've never even heard of."

Patsy smacked her lips. "Dang! Maybe living here won't be so bad after all!"

chapter four

The girls ended up spending most of the weekend together, playing games, unpacking Patsy's clothes and putting them in drawers, having bike races up and down the alley, eating Fudgsicles, and enjoying their new friendship. Patsy was a little bit of a show-off, Juliet thought, but she was so much fun to play with that Juliet figured she could overlook it.

The only thing that would have made the weekend better was if Lowell had been around to notice her enjoying her new friend, but Juliet never saw him, even though she looked for him every time she went outside. She told herself it didn't matter anymore—she had a new friend, a better friend than Lowell. But as much as she liked Patsy, a new friend was not as comfortable as an old one. She'd eaten a hundred meals at Lowell's house, and he at hers. She was used to his soft-spoken parents, and he was no longer shaken by an argument at the Klostermeyer supper table. After six years they knew everything about each other. How could that not matter anymore?

Sunday night Juliet and Caroline's mother made her usual nighttime visit to their room at nine o'clock. "Lights out, girls. School day tomorrow."

Juliet put the *Wonder Woman* comic book on the table beside her bed.

"I don't see why I have to go to bed so early just because Juliet is a baby," Caroline complained, but she put her *Seventeen* magazine aside too and turned out the lamp between the two beds.

They settled down under their quilts, and Juliet started her nightly prayers. She did them after the lights were out so Caroline wouldn't suspect. Juliet didn't want her sister asking nosy questions about what she was praying for.

Dear God, I would appreciate it if you could get the Russians to calm down and stop making bombs. They could start a war that would wreck the whole world! If you really made the world, you wouldn't want it all ruined, would you?

Caroline interrupted her thoughts. "So, are you friends with that Patsy girl now?"

"Yeah. What do you care?"

"I don't. Except that she's weird."

"She is not!" Juliet yelled.

"Shut up! You'll get Mom back in here," Caroline warned.

"Patsy is not weird," Juliet whispered.

"She's got weird hair. And she acts tough, like she's a big

tomboy or something. Mimi's mother heard her yelling at Bruce Wagner the other day. She said Patsy cursed at him!"

"She did not! I was right there. She called him a nose-bleed is all."

"Well, that's bad enough," Caroline said. "Why would anybody want to get Bruce Wagner mad at them? He even scares me, and I'm two years older than him."

"You're scared of your shadow," Juliet said.

"Me? You're the big chicken!"

"Not as big as you!"

"Okay!" Mom yelled from downstairs. "Be quiet and go to sleep. If I have to come up there, you'll both be sorry!"

Juliet gave her sister a nasty look that Caroline couldn't see and went back to her prayers.

Dear God, I wish you could help me figure out why Lowell doesn't want to be my friend anymore. And also I'd like to stop missing him so much, because he's a big louse. And one more thing: Even though my dad is older than my mom, if there is any way that they could both live for about a hundred years, I would really appreciate it. If you don't have time to keep Caroline alive, we could probably get along without her.

In the morning Patsy's mother drove them to school. The girls planned to ride their bikes other mornings, but since it was Patsy and David's first day, Mrs. Osgood had to go to the office to get them registered.

"If the principal wants somebody to show you around," Juliet said, "be sure to tell her that you already know me and I'll do it!"

"Okay!" Patsy waved to Juliet and followed her mother down the hall.

As class started, Juliet watched the door nervously. Finally, Mrs. Hoover came into their classroom with Patsy behind her.

"Mrs. Funkhauser, here's your new student. Class, I'd like you to say hello to Patricia Marie Osgood."

Everybody sat up straight in their chairs and stared at Patsy. A few kids mumbled "hello" so you could barely hear it, so Juliet yelled out, "Hi, Patsy!" to make up for everybody else who didn't. She waved her arm in the air, too, in case there was anyone who didn't realize that Patsy was *hers*.

"Apparently," said Mrs. Hoover, "Juliet Klostermeyer has already met our new student, so we'll let her do the honors of showing Patricia around today." Then she looked at Mrs. Funkhauser and said, "Let me know if there are any problems."

Mrs. Funkhauser nodded back, and the two of them stared at each other for a minute as if they were passing a secret message back and forth with their eyes. Then Mrs. Funkhauser gave Patsy a desk in Juliet's row, just two seats back. Too far for whispering, but at least they could smile and wave.

Juliet was so excited she could barely listen to the geography lesson and got quite a few of the products mixed up on the map of South America. Math was horribly boring, and Juliet was bouncing in her seat by the time Mrs. Funkhauser marched the class down to the cafeteria for lunch.

"This place is really different from my school in Tucson," Patsy said as they walked down the hall together.

"How?"

"Well, for one thing, this building is so old. We had a real new school in Tucson."

Juliet had never thought of the Jefferson School as old, even though she knew that her mother had gone there too.

"And in Tucson we did South America in fourth grade, so now I have to do it *again*. In fifth grade in Tucson you do Australia, which is better, because they have kangaroos. And your teacher, Funkenbush or whoever she is, is terrible."

Even though Juliet wasn't crazy about Mrs. Funkhauser herself, there were things about her that she was starting to appreciate, like the way she wasn't all that strict about talking, and how she let kids work on projects in groups. She wasn't *terrible*. Juliet was getting a little tired of hearing about how much better everything was in Tucson.

When they entered the cafeteria, Patsy stopped in the

doorway to survey the room. "So, who do you sit with?" she asked.

"Over there, those two girls with the ponytails. You'll like them," Juliet said, although she wasn't really sure Patsy would.

"Hi," Juliet said as she plunked her lunch box on the table. "This is Patsy. She just moved in down the street from me."

"You're the new girl," Annette said, as if Patsy weren't aware of the fact. "I'm Annette and she's Linda."

"Where'd you move here from?" Linda wanted to know.

"Tucson," Patsy said. She opened her brown bag and dug right in, getting out a bologna sandwich, an apple, and half a dozen Oreo cookies. She unscrewed the cap of her thermos and took a big gulp of milk.

"I've heard of Tucson," Linda said. "Where is it again?"

"Arizona," Juliet answered, because Patsy was still drinking.

"Arizona? Isn't that a desert or something?" Annette asked. "Do they have cactuses there?"

"Yup," Patsy said. She bit into her sandwich and kept on talking. "But Tucson is a big city. *Much* bigger than this little place."

Linda and Annette gave each other looks; Juliet figured

they didn't like Patsy calling Wisdom Hill a "little place," even though it was.

"Patsy's dad got transferred to Lathrop," Juliet said, trying to get the conversation on another track.

Annette nodded her head knowingly. "Air Force brat, huh?"

"And proud of it!" Patsy said, sinking her teeth into the flesh of her apple.

"Is your dad a pilot?" Linda asked.

Patsy gave Juliet a look, and for a moment Juliet wondered if Patsy was going to lie and say he was, but then she sighed. "He's a mechanic. He fixes planes."

Linda and Annette had no response to this news. They pulled the crusts off their peanut butter sandwiches.

"But when I grow up, *I'm* going to be a pilot," Patsy said. "I already decided. I'll go to the Air Force Academy in Colorado to learn how."

That got the attention of all three girls.

"Really?" Juliet said.

"I don't think girls *can* fly planes," Annette said.

"Sure they can," Patsy said. "Why couldn't they?"

"They can't join the Air Force, can they?" Linda asked.

"Yes, they can. I looked it up."

"They can't go to war, though, and that's what they need the pilots for," Annette said, poking her hard-boiled egg at Patsy. "They aren't going to teach a girl how to fly a plane if she can't even go to war."

Patsy scowled and juggled her half-eaten apple between her two hands. Juliet hoped she wouldn't throw it at Annette.

"So, what did you guys do this weekend?" Juliet asked, trying to get the group on a better footing.

Linda shrugged. "Not much. I had to go visit my grandparents in St. Louis. It's so boring there—they don't even have a television."

"Why don't you take a book?" Annette suggested.

"I *do*, but how many hours can you just sit and read?"

Now Annette and Linda were acting more normal, and Juliet sighed with relief. "What did you do, Annette?"

"Saturday afternoon I went with my dad and my brother to the go-kart track." She raised her eyebrows and giggled. "Your friend Lowell was there."

Juliet's face froze. "He's not my friend anymore. He's got new friends now."

"Yeah, they were with him. Mike and Tommy Lambert." She turned to Linda. "Don't you think Mike Lambert is just a doll?"

"He's really cute," Linda agreed. "For twins they don't look much alike, do they? Tommy is so skinny, but Mike is . . ."

"Adorable!" Annette said.

Juliet looked at Patsy and shrugged. Patsy passed her an Oreo.

"I don't like either one of them," Juliet said. "They're over at Lowell's all the time, working on that stupid go-kart like it's a real car or something."

"You're just mad because they stole your boyfriend away," Linda said, laughing.

Which made Juliet furious. "Lowell is *not* my boyfriend! How many times do I have to tell you?"

Linda shook her head. "I'm just teasing you, Juliet."

Annette reached over and grabbed Linda's arm. "You know what? We could go over to Juliet's house and watch them work on the go-kart! Could we, Juliet? I really want to talk to Mike!"

"You want to come over just so you can meet Mike Lambert? That is so stupid."

"No, it's not! Please!" Annette begged.

"They won't even talk to you," Juliet said. "They don't like girls."

Annette pouted. "You're just saying that because you don't like boys."

"Patsy, have *you* ever had a boyfriend?" Linda asked.

Patsy screwed up her face into a goofy grin. "Well, there was this one boy who liked me last year," she said. "He was pretty boss."

Annette and Linda both squealed. "Tell us!"

And even though Juliet knew she ought to be happy that Annette and Linda had found something to like about Patsy, instead she thought, *Why am I the only girl that boys don't like?*

"This boy, Pablo," Patsy said. "He was a year ahead of me. He wanted me to go over his house and watch television with him."

"Did you?" Annette leaned over the table to listen.

Patsy used a fingernail to dig out a chunk of chocolate cookie from between her front teeth. "Nah. I punched him in the face instead." Her laugh resounded across the cafeteria, and Mrs. Funkhauser turned around to see who was making all the noise.

Annette and Linda threw their leftovers into their lunch boxes and parceled out very disdainful looks to Patsy and Juliet as they headed for the girls' bathroom. Apparently, they did not appreciate Patsy's sense of humor as much as Juliet did.

chapter five

Juliet was lying on her bed with an *Archie* comic book open in front of her, but she wasn't really reading it. Memories of her grandfather had stolen into her mind, as they often did during quiet moments, and she was remembering summer a year ago—more than a year now—when she and her grandfather spent long afternoons working in his vegetable garden.

As they staked the tomatoes and tied the string bean vines to the trellis, Grandpa would make up stories about "the tender little tomato," who cried about everything, and her annoying friend, "the tattletale tomato," who complained about everything. His voice leaped from a high whine to a low grumble as the two tomatoes argued about life in the garden.

"Oh, the marigolds look so thirsty," Tender would say. "I'm worried that Grandpa has forgotten them!"

"Worry about *us*, why dontcha?" Tattletale would answer. "That old man's been known to pick a tomato before it was even ripe!"

Sometimes Grandpa made the string beans dance together, the long skinny pods swinging into a jerky waltz. Then he'd let Juliet climb up on his big rubber boots, and he'd dance her down the rows between the leeks and the broccoli. No one was more fun than Grandpa.

How, she asked herself for the hundredth time, could he be gone? Disappeared? She'd asked God if he knew where her grandpa was, but she hadn't really expected an answer, and none had come.

What she really wanted to know was why people had to die at all. You spent so many years learning how to live; it seemed like a huge waste that once you'd figured it all out—memorized the multiplication tables and learned to grow tomatoes and make birdhouses—after all of that growing up, death came along and took it all away. Why even bother to go to school and learn things? Especially now, when the Russian president, Khrushchev, banged his shoe on a table and threatened to "bury" the United States? She might not even live as long as her grandpa had.

But thinking about that made Juliet's stomach hurt, so she turned back to her comic book again. At least with Patsy around all week she hadn't had time to dwell on such things as much. But that afternoon Patsy's mother had insisted on taking both her children downtown to buy them boots and coats, which they hadn't needed in Arizona but would certainly need for an Illinois winter. The timing was bad, because Caroline and Mimi were staying late after school to paint sets for a play, so the younger girls could have had the room to themselves without an argument.

"Juliet! I need you!" her mother called up the stairs. "I've got a job for you."

Wouldn't you know, as soon as Juliet had a minute to herself, her mother would find some chore to use it up on?

"I'm reading," Juliet called down the stairs, even though she knew Ethel did not consider reading a valid excuse for dodging work. Especially reading a comic book.

"Come down here now. You can read anytime."

Anytime my mother isn't around, Juliet thought. Reluctantly, she swung her legs off the bed and plodded down the stairs. Wouldn't it be nice if her mother were calling her downstairs to suggest that the two of them drive downtown to sit at the Woolworth's counter and have a malt together? Or to go out to the new miniature golf course that had just opened and play a game or two? But that kind of thing never happened. Ethel would say it was a waste of precious time.

"What job?" Juliet asked.

"I need you to go out to the dog pen and sort through the soda bottle returns. They need to be grouped by the distributor that picks them up. I'll give you a list of what goes with what."

"That's Caroline's job!"

"Well, Caroline's busy these days. Besides, you're old enough now. And I pay her a dollar to do it, you know."

A dollar was nothing to sneeze at; until she was old enough to babysit, there weren't many ways for her to earn spending money. She took the list her mother handed her, pulled on a jacket, and went out the back door.

"Put the broken glass in the garbage can. And don't cut yourself!" her mother yelled after her. "And throw away any bottle caps you find too—the distributors don't want them back."

Her parents called the fenced area off the garage the "dog pen," even though they'd never had a dog to put in it themselves. Apparently, the previous owners had had an enormous animal, though, because the wooden fence was a good six feet high. Juliet dragged a heavy trash barrel around to the front of the pen, unlocked the gate, and stepped inside.

What a mess. Even though the gate was kept locked, sometimes neighborhood kids scaled the fence and threw the bottles around just for the heck of it. Juliet figured Bruce Wagner was a prime suspect. There were a few broken bottles on the floor of the pen, but most of them were just dumped out of their cardboard cartons and scattered around.

Juliet studied her list. A&W root beer was by itself

in one corner. Hires root beer was stacked with the Vess bottles: orange, grape, and cream soda, all together. Pepsi went with Bubble-Up and Royal Crown. Coke went with 7-Up and Dr Pepper—that took up one whole side of the pen—and Squirt was by itself. She'd have to get the unbroken bottles back in their cartons and stacked up before she could pick up the bottle caps and broken pieces of glass beneath them.

The work wasn't hard; it was even kind of pleasant, if sticky. Juliet had always enjoyed putting things in order. She was the kind of girl who kept her books alphabetized and her hair barrettes arranged by color. Stacking soda bottles was just another way of setting the world straight, and she did a good job of it. Although she would never admit it to Caroline, she found herself singing one of her sister's favorite songs, a tune called "Duke of Earl" by Gene Chandler, over and over to herself. Juliet thought the words were stupid, but she liked the song anyway.

She was just about to open the gate and prop it with the garbage can when someone knocked on it. Her mother? She wouldn't knock.

Juliet opened the gate carefully, part of her afraid she'd find Bruce Wagner standing there, ready to pounce on her. But instead it was Lowell on the other side of the fence, his hands stuffed in his pockets, scuffing the gravel of the alley with his tennis shoes.

Juliet was shocked into silence; he was the last person she'd expected to see. Lowell's tongue didn't seem to be operational either. He peered at her with eyes that looked ready to dart away at any minute.

Finally, he muttered, "I saw you come in here. You sorting bottles?"

She nodded. "I'm almost done. Just picking up broken glass and bottle caps."

"Need any help?"

She'd been in there for forty-five minutes already. If he'd seen her come in and wanted to help her, why'd it take him so long to come over?

"Where are your *friends*?" she asked him in a disagreeable voice.

Lowell looked at the ground. "They had to go to the dentist today."

"Oh." Juliet hoped they'd each have to have a few teeth pulled, but she refrained from saying so. "I guess you can help me if you want to."

Lowell stepped into the pen, and Juliet stuck the garbage can in the doorway so they could throw the debris right into it. Even though Juliet had been wanting to hang around with Lowell for weeks, now that he was actually here she didn't know what to say to him. Everything was different from before.

The dog pen wasn't very big to begin with, and all the

stacked bottles took up a lot of space around the outside edges, so the two of them had to be careful not to bump into each other when they bent down to pick things up. Juliet wasn't sure exactly why she didn't want to bump into Lowell—a month ago it wouldn't have been any big deal—but she was aware that Lowell felt the same way about it that she did. Maybe they weren't good enough friends to bump into each other anymore; if they did, they might have to apologize, and that would be really weird. They worked cautiously and in silence until everything but the slivers was in the garbage.

"Okay, we're done," Juliet said. She rubbed her sticky hands on the sides of her blue jeans.

"Okay," Lowell said. He didn't leave the pen, though—he just stood there, staring at the ground. Juliet finally stepped around him. She wasn't going to stand there all day.

"Juliet!" Lowell grabbed her arm as she started to leave.

"What?" Her voice came out in a bark.

He dropped her arm like it was a log on fire. "I just wanted to say, you know, I feel kind of bad about, you know."

Juliet felt her face grow hot, and words began to bubble out of her like lava running downhill. "You mean you feel bad about the way you don't talk to me anymore? And the way you and your new friends don't want me around? You don't act like you feel bad about it, Lowell. You act like you're happy as a pig in mud that you don't have to play with a *girl* anymore." Juliet stepped out of the dog pen, jerked the garbage can away from the gate, and let it crash closed behind her.

Lowell pushed through the gate, and the two of them stood glaring at each other over the garbage can.

"You don't get it," Lowell said, gritting his teeth.

"I get it. Your new friends think I'm going to give them girl cooties."

"That's not true. They just aren't used to playing with girls. They think girls are sissies and don't like to fix cars and stuff."

"I *don't* like to fix cars—and you never did either. And I'm not a sissy!" She stopped herself before she said that of the two of them *he* was the bigger sissy.

"I know you're not."

"Well, can't you tell them I'm not?"

Lowell kicked the garbage can hard. "Juliet, they just think what they think! Besides, we're getting too old to be best friends. You have to play with girls and I have to play with boys."

"Says who? There's no rule!"

"Mike and Tommy think there is, and if I want to be their friend . . . well . . . I can't be your friend."

Juliet blinked her eyes, praying no tears would leak out

in front of this traitor. "That's the dumbest thing I ever heard."

Lowell looked off down the alley as if checking to see if anyone was watching them. "Aren't you friends with that new girl now? I see you riding bikes with her all the time."

Juliet sniffed. At least he knew she wasn't sitting around all day waiting for him to show up. "Her name is Patsy. She lives right down on Boxfield Road and she's my new best friend."

"Well, see, it's okay then. You have a girl to play with, and I have boys. That's how it's supposed to work." Lowell's mouth moved into a hesitant smile. "Isn't it?"

Juliet said nothing. She grabbed the heavy metal can and started to pull it back around the side of the building.

"Well, isn't it?" Lowell shouted. "I don't see why you're so mad!"

Juliet stopped and turned around to glare at her former best friend. The words that had been on the tip of her tongue for weeks came spitting out.

"I hate you, Lowell McManus. I hate you forever."

Lowell looked stunned, as if she'd hit him with a rock instead of words. It took him a minute to collect himself, but then his face hardened.

"Fine. Then I hate you, too," he said, and walked away.

chapter six

On Saturday morning Juliet and Patsy were sitting on the front step of Klostermeyer's Market, having just been banished from Juliet's room by Caroline and Mimi, who demanded privacy in order to discuss the previous evening's high school football game.

"Your mom is really neat, isn't she?" Juliet said, staring into space.

Patsy shrugged. "I don't know. Is she?"

"Yeah! I mean, she does stuff with you and David all the time. And when I come over, she sits down and talks to me. And she baked us brownies yesterday before we even asked for a snack!"

"All mothers do stuff like that."

"Not mine," Juliet said. "She never has the time."

"Well, your mom works in the store all day. Besides, she lets us take Twinkies almost anytime we want to."

"That's different. She doesn't *make* the Twinkies."

Patsy wrinkled up her nose. "So?"

"I don't know." Juliet was having a hard time explaining,

even to herself, why those homemade brownies had made her feel so deprived. She understood that her mother had no choice but to work in the store. They couldn't afford to hire someone else to do the work she did.

But how did it turn out like that? Patsy's mom didn't work. Lowell's mom didn't work. In fact the only kid she could think of whose mother worked was Bruce Wagner. But his mom was divorced, and besides, she probably couldn't wait to get away from her rotten son.

"So, where should we ride our bikes?" Patsy asked. "The comic book store?" But before Juliet could answer, Annette Hendricks and Linda Wheeler came sauntering down Abbott Street with big grins on their faces, their ponytails swinging in unison.

"What are *they* doing here?" Patsy asked.

"I don't know. They haven't come to my house in ages," Juliet said.

Annette and Linda waved as they approached. "Hey, you two!" Annette yelled happily. "Whatcha doin'?"

"Nothing," Juliet said. "What are you doing here?"

"We just came by to see what you guys were doing," Annette said in a loud, singsong voice.

"Yeah," Linda said. "It's so *boring* at our houses."

"We're going for a bike ride," Patsy said. "There's this comic book store where they let you trade in your old comics and get new ones for half price."

Juliet knew that idea wasn't going to interest these two.

Annette rolled her eyes. "Comic books are for little kids. Wouldn't you rather meet Juliet's neighbor? He and his friends are right over there!"

"Where?" Patsy wanted to know. But Juliet didn't have to ask. She had radar for Lowell's whereabouts, more now than ever. She couldn't see him from the step where she sat, but she'd heard the boys' growly voices and the whine of the go-kart engine the minute they came outside.

Juliet shrugged. "Go over if you want, but I'm not going with you, if that's what you think. I'm not speaking to Lowell anymore."

"Oh, come on, Juliet. Just walk over with us and then you can leave," Annette begged. "I don't really know Lowell, and he'll think it's weird if I just suddenly drop by."

"He'll think it's even weirder if I drop by, believe me," Juliet said.

Linda looked crestfallen. "I wore my new jacket and tennis shoes so I'd look good," she said.

Patsy snorted. "Boys don't care about stuff like that." She got up from the step and walked down the sidewalk so she could look across the alley. "Which one is Lowell?"

"Shhh!" Juliet motioned to Patsy to get back. "Do you want them to think we're talking about them?"

"I don't care," Annette said. "Lowell is the short one in the blue jacket, with the blondish hair. The boys with the dark hair are Mike and Tommy Lambert. Mike is the cute one."

"There are four of them," Patsy said. "There's a kid in the back, just sitting there, not helping."

"Oh, they see us looking at them!" Linda said, bouncing on her toes.

"I told you!" Juliet said. "Stop looking!"

"We might as well go over now," Annette said. "They know we're talking about them anyway."

"I'm not going over there!" Juliet repeated.

"Yeah, let's go over," Patsy said.

Juliet stared at Patsy. "What? Why do *you* want to go?"

"I wanna meet this jerk, Lowell, who used to be your best friend. I wanna see what makes him so special."

"Nothing makes him special!" Juliet said, but Patsy had grabbed her by the arm and hauled her to her feet, and the four of them seemed to be heading toward Lowell's yard whether she wanted to or not. She tried at first to pull away, but the boys were looking at them, and struggling seemed more embarrassing than just going along with it.

"Fine, but I'm just going to introduce you and leave," Juliet said, wishing she could disappear.

The four girls trudged across the lawn toward the carport, Patsy in the lead, pulling Juliet, with Annette and Linda, who'd been so eager to do this to begin with, hanging back shyly. Juliet shook herself free of Patsy's hand and then stopped dead in her tracks, so that Linda bumped into her from behind. She had just made eye contact with the mysterious fourth boy and realized it was Bruce Wagner.

Patsy seemed to recognize him too, and Bruce certainly remembered her. He stood up from the lawn chair and looked straight at her. "What are *you* doing here? Who invited you over?"

"You don't live here," she answered back. "This isn't your property—you can't kick me off."

"Gosh!" Annette stepped forward, her confidence suddenly restored. "Nobody said anything about kicking anybody off of anything, Patsy! Don't have a cow! Juliet just wanted us all to come over and meet all of you. Right, Juliet?"

But Juliet couldn't move her mouth or even shake her head. Lowell was staring at her now, his eyes cold and slitted. This was absolutely the last place on earth she wanted to be.

Linda stepped in to cover the silence. "We know that you two are new at school," she said, nodding toward Mike and Tommy, who were acting as though the girls were invisible, "and, well, Patsy here is new too, and we thought we should all get to know each other. I mean, since we're all in fifth grade and everything."

"I'm not in fifth grade," Bruce said, spitting out the word "fifth" as if it were poisonous.

Annette and Linda smiled halfheartedly. They knew quite well who Bruce Wagner was—everybody at Jefferson School did. He wasn't part of their plans for the day, but now that he was here, he couldn't be ignored.

Juliet hadn't seen Bruce close up for a while and she was surprised to see a rash of red pimples blooming on his cheeks and forehead. Just what he needs, she thought—something to make him look even meaner.

But a bigger shock was seeing Bruce at Lowell's house. Why would he be here? Bruce always made fun of Lowell and called him a sissy or a pansy; Juliet was quite certain they'd never spoken a pleasant word to each other. Maybe it had something to do with the go-kart. Or maybe the Lamberts invited him. Juliet tried to catch Lowell's eye to see if he seemed worried or scared, but he was making himself look busy, stirring up a can of paint as if it were a terribly important job he had to get just right.

Mike Lambert finally put down the wrench he was using to tighten a bolt and looked up at Patsy. "So, is your dad a pilot too?" he asked.

Patsy gave him a sour look. "No. I guess yours is?"

Mike nodded.

Annette filled in the missing information. "Patsy's father is a mechanic."

"Yeah!" Patsy said. "Your dad wouldn't have anything to fly in if my dad didn't keep the planes working!"

Mike seemed unimpressed. Bruce Wagner laughed. "Big deal. Anybody can fix an airplane—you have to be *smart* to fly 'em."

Patsy started to sputter, but Annette cut her off. "So, what are you guys doing, anyway? Can we help?"

Tommy Lambert spoke up then. "Do you know anything about go-karts?"

"Of course they don't!" Bruce interrupted. "Are you kidding me? They're girls! All they know about is dumb girl stuff."

Patsy shoved past Annette and right into Bruce's face. "I know plenty about go-karts! And car engines too! I also know you're an idiot. Anybody can*not* fix an airplane, and girls can do anything boys can do! And if you insult my father again, I'm gonna pound you."

Bruce laughed. "Listen, dogface, I already know you think you're a big tough tomboy, but don't think I wouldn't hit a girl, because I darn well would."

Finally, Lowell looked up from the paint can. "Hold on, now. Nobody is hitting anybody. We're just working on the go-kart." He turned to look at Juliet, but his eyes skidded off her face and landed on Patsy's instead. "You girls should probably leave now."

Juliet wanted very badly to leave, but the idea that Lowell was *telling* them to go made her stand her ground. The other girls didn't move either.

"We *would* be working on the go-kart if you'd ever get the stupid paint stirred up," Bruce growled. "Whaddaya think you're doin' over there, makin' a cake?"

Juliet noticed Mike and Tommy trade a look; she decided they weren't too crazy about Bruce either. Why didn't they say something? Were they all scared of him?

"I've got the brushes," Tommy said, and started passing them around.

"I can paint really good," Linda said. "I do paint-by-numbers all the time."

"Yeah, I do too," Annette said, not to be left out.

"You only did that one," Linda reminded her.

"Well, still," she said. "I know how to paint!"

"Look," Lowell said. "Cars are something boys work on, not girls."

"Yeah," Bruce agreed. "Even the pantywaist knows that much—don'tcha, Lowell? There's boy stuff and there's girl stuff, and they aren't the same. So beat it."

"Since when?" Juliet was suddenly yelling—at Lowell, not Bruce. "Since when is there 'boy stuff' and 'girl stuff'?" Lowell certainly hadn't seen any difference between the two for the past six years!

"Yeah! And just what do you think is 'girl stuff'?" Patsy said.

"I'll tell you what 'girl stuff' is, dogface," Bruce

yelled back at Patsy, running a hand through his choppy haircut. "It's painting your fingernails red and brushing each other's hair. It's sittin' on your butt, playing stupid games and reading books. It's bein' scared of your own shadow!"

Juliet saw the other boys' faces get red, probably because they didn't use words like "butt" in front of girls. She figured Lowell was also blushing because he'd spent plenty of time in his life playing games and reading books, just like she had. And he probably wondered if she remembered how scared he'd gotten the one night last year that they'd been allowed to stay up and watch *Spook Spectacular* on television; Juliet had had to walk him back across the alley afterward because he was too frightened to walk home in the dark by himself.

"That's not all girls do," Patsy said. "We ride bikes and we play baseball and we run just as fast as boys do. And I never even brush my *own* hair!"

But Bruce ignored her. "And girls sew little dresses for their dollies, and they have tea parties with their mommies, and they–"

"I never had a tea party in my life!" Patsy said. "You don't know what you're talking about! Girls can do anything boys can do! At least *I* can!"

The other three boys had begun slathering blue paint on the go-kart, but they stopped and looked up at Patsy, then at Bruce, as if they knew what was coming.

"Oh, really?" Bruce said, digging a finger in his ear. "Anything, huh? Is that a challenge?"

"Yeah, it's a challenge!" Patsy said. "I can do anything you can do, and I can do it *better*, too!"

Bruce stared at Patsy for a minute or so, an evil grin spreading across his face. Juliet knew she ought to take Patsy's arm and drag her back across the lawn to Klostermeyer's Market, but there was a part of her that loved watching Patsy stand up to that crazy Bruce Wagner and not even look scared.

Bruce flopped back down into the lawn chair and stretched his long legs out in front of him; he obviously had no intention of helping the others paint the go-kart. "Okay, then. Let's set up some tests. One test a day, starting today and ending, say, next weekend." He counted on his fingers. "Nine tests. Boys against the girls. Whichever side wins the most tests is the winner of the challenge. Of course, if we win the first five, you can just give up." Mike and Tommy laughed, but nervously.

Girls? Plural? Juliet started to sweat beneath her jacket. *She* wasn't challenging Bruce Wagner.

"Fine," Patsy said. "The four of us against the four of you."

"What?" Lowell put down his brush. "What kind of tests?"

"Yeah, what kind of tests?" Linda wanted to know. She looked nervously at Annette. "I've got my good tennis shoes on, and if I get them dirty . . ."

"Oh, the girls can't get dirty. Well, I guess you forfeit, then," Bruce said, laughing.

"We do not forfeit!" Patsy glared at Linda. "Come on. We can beat them. God, I could probably beat 'em all by myself!"

"Tell you what," Bruce said. "You girls can come up with the first test. After that, whoever wins gets to make up the next one. That's fair, isn't it?"

"Are you gonna do it, Mike?" Annette said, smiling sweetly at his ruddy, paint-streaked cheeks.

Mike blushed again. "I don't know. I guess."

"Then I will too. Come on, Linda," Annette begged her friend. "It'll be fun. Or at least it won't be boring!"

Linda didn't look convinced, but she said, "Well, I guess, if you think we should."

Patsy turned to Juliet. "You in?"

Juliet nodded. The idea of going head to head with Bruce Wagner in any kind of test scared the gravy out of her, but she wasn't going to show it in front of Lowell. Besides, Lowell was no great athlete—she was better at most physical stuff than he was. Juliet was certain she could at least show *him* up, and that was worth getting clobbered by Bruce.

"Okay, we're on, then," Bruce said. The other three boys hadn't actually agreed to anything, but Juliet knew they didn't have a choice. "So, girls get to pick the first test. What'll it be?"

chapter seven

Patsy assumed the role of captain for the girls' team without a vote being taken, but without any complaints, either. The four of them went back to Juliet's yard to discuss privately what the first test should be. As they left Lowell's property, they heard Bruce bellowing, "This'll be a cinch. Girls got no guts. We'll clobber 'em!"

"Somebody needs to teach that jerk a lesson," Patsy grumbled. It was clear to all the girls that Patsy was eager to take on the job.

"I can't believe Lowell is letting Bruce hang out in his yard," Juliet said. "He hates Bruce."

"Lowell doesn't seem like the kind of kid who stands up to people," Patsy said.

"Yeah," Annette said. "Lowell is really nice."

Juliet snorted. "He is *not* nice. He used to be nice, but now he's just as crummy as any other boy."

Since Linda was so worried about messing up her sneakers, they tried to think of a contest which would be more or less clean. Patsy, however, was not pleased to have to take this requirement into consideration.

"They're *shoes*," she said. "They're supposed to get dirty. You better wear old stuff tomorrow. We have to be able to get as dirty as they do."

But Linda was worried about the whole situation. "I can't believe we're really going to do this for nine days. I'll probably come in last every time."

"Who cares?" Annette said. "We'll get to hang around with Mike and Tommy for over a week—by that time we'll be their friends. In fact they'll like us even better if we *don't* win."

"I can't believe you said that!" Patsy glared at Annette disgustedly. "You're just doing this so the boys will *like* you?"

Annette wound her ponytail around her finger. "I came over here to *meet* Mike Lambert, not to beat him up; you're the one who set this whole challenge thing up. Just because you don't like being a girl—"

"I never said that! Just because I'm a girl doesn't mean I have to be a quiet little priss who can't get her clothes dirty."

Linda pouted. "If you don't want us to be on your team, we'll go home. You can find somebody else to do your silly tests."

"Look," Juliet said. "I don't really want to do this either, but I don't like the way they talk about girls. We're not scaredy-cats and sissies. We're just as good as they are, and we should prove it to them."

Patsy grabbed a low-hanging tree branch and ripped the yellow leaves off of it. "If you two give up and let the boys win without even trying, you'll be very sorry. That's all I have to say: You'll be very sorry."

Annette and Linda exchanged worried glances, then promised, reluctantly, to do their best.

"Okay, then. I think the first test should be a race," Patsy said. "I'm a *really* fast runner. I always beat the boys at my school in Tucson."

"*All* the boys?" Annette asked.

"Maybe not every boy every time, but, believe me, they knew I *could* beat 'em."

"I know I can beat Lowell," Juliet said. "He's a terrible runner. But I think Bruce might be fast. I don't know about the others."

"I can beat Bruce," Patsy declared. "I *will* beat Bruce."

The other two girls agreed that a race would be fine. After all, anybody could run a block or two. It wouldn't last that long, and it wouldn't damage Linda's shoes.

Patsy came up with the scoring method, and when they walked back over to Lowell's, she explained it to the boys, who were cleaning the blue paint out of their brushes under the hose spigot.

"The winner gets five points, second place gets four, third

place gets three, fourth gets two, and fifth gets one. The last three get nothing. We add it up and see who wins."

Bruce agreed, and the other boys nodded their heads, Lowell unenthusiastically. "We'll run on Grove Street," Bruce said. "We need chalk to mark off the beginning and the end. And we need somebody to start us and somebody to stand at the finish line in case it's close. I mean, I'll win, but the second, third, and fourth places might be close."

Juliet saw Lowell roll his eyes in disgust. At least he hadn't changed *that* much. If her oldest friend had suddenly decided he liked this person who'd tormented them for years, she'd know for sure the world was too unpredictable to count on anything.

"Who can we get to do that?" Lowell dared to ask. "This is everybody our age in the neighborhood."

"Is your mom home?" Patsy asked Lowell.

"I'm not asking my mom," Lowell said firmly. "She's too busy to do something like this."

And besides, Juliet thought, *you don't want her to see you lose to a bunch of girls.*

"I guess I could ask my sister and her friend," Juliet said, when it became obvious there was no one else to do it. "But I'm not guaranteeing anything. They don't like to go outside unless the house is on fire."

"Get 'em," Bruce commanded. "There's nobody else. They gotta do it."

But Caroline and Mimi were not easy to convince. "You're having a race against boys?" Caroline had said. "That's the dumbest thing I ever heard of. Everybody knows boys can run faster."

It was only when Juliet mentioned that Annette Hendricks was one of the other girls that they became interested.

"That's Robby Hendricks's little sister," Mimi said. "She's adorable!"

"I can't believe you talked her into this," Caroline said.

"I didn't talk her into it. She wants to hang around with this new boy, Mike Lambert, who's on the other team."

"Oh, isn't that cute?" Mimi said. The two of them eventually decided to come out of the bedroom in order to protect Annette from Juliet and Patsy's stupid scheme and also to get a look at this Mike Lambert kid who adorable little Annette had a crush on.

By the time they got back outside, Lowell had come up with a piece of chalk, and Bruce had marked off the starting and finish lines at each end of the street. Tommy Lambert was telling elephant jokes while they waited.

"What's gray and white on the inside and red and white on the outside?"

"Tell us," Mike said.

"Campbells's Cream of Elephant soup!"

Mike groaned. Linda said, "That's a good one."

Bruce gave her a sour look. "Elephant jokes are stupid,"

he said. "We got judges now—let's start the race."

Mimi took the starting line and Caroline trudged up to the finish, but not before she pulled Juliet aside to say, "What is Bruce Wagner doing here? You didn't tell me he was involved in this!"

The eight of them lined up, girl-boy-girl-boy, across the width of the street. Patsy instructed them to each put their right toe at the starting line, but Bruce yelled back that the boys could start any old way they wanted to. "You guys," he said, "pretend there's a Commie chasing you and the finish line is your bunker. You get across fast or you're dead!"

Mimi called the start, and they took off at more or less the same time. Patsy pulled out in front immediately, her legs churning the air and beating the pavement, her face fixed in a determined scowl. But Bruce Wagner was not far behind her, and his longer legs covered the distance more easily. Juliet herself was only a little farther back, but she was running so hard, so fast, that after the first minute she couldn't get her breath, and she knew she wouldn't be able to go at that speed the whole way. *At least I'm ahead of Lowell,* she thought, *and I'm going to keep it that way.*

She saw her sister standing at the finish line but wasn't sure just who she was rooting for as she leaped up and down. Mike Lambert came up beside Juliet and passed her with only a few yards to go. She gasped for breath, willed her legs to keep moving, and threw herself across the finish line, then staggered to the curb to lie back on the sidewalk and catch her breath. For a moment she didn't care who'd won; she was just happy to have done it and to have done it as well as she could.

In a second Caroline was standing over her. "I didn't know you could run that fast! You beat two of the boys!"

Two? Juliet thought. *Was that good enough?* She sat up slowly and looked around her. The boys were all still on their feet, puffing and walking in circles. Annette was lying on the grass, and Linda was holding her side, tears streaming down her cheeks. Patsy strode up to Caroline. She did not look pleased.

"Okay, what was the final order?"

"Bruce won." The boys hollered like crazy. "You came in second, Patsy." The girls yelled, but with less enthusiasm and without Linda. "Then it was Mike, Juliet, Tommy, Annette, Lowell, and Linda."

Even Annette had beaten Lowell. Juliet knew that was a blow, and she would almost have felt sorry for him, except that when Bruce screamed, "Boys win, nine to five!" Lowell jumped around and pounded his teammates on the back as hard as all the other boys did, as if he'd had something to do with their victory.

Patsy scowled at them. "Nine to *six*, idiot. Can't you even add?"

"Who cares? We won!" Mike shouted.

Bruce stuck out his tongue at Patsy. "Tomorrow's test is our choice," he reminded them.

Patsy looked glum but said, "We'll be here. What time?"

"You aren't really going to keep doing this, are you?" Caroline asked Juliet.

"Yes!" Juliet hissed.

"I have to go to church in the morning," Linda said, her tears finally dried up.

"Me too," Annette said. "I sing in the choir."

"So does Lowell," Juliet said. She thought she was just stating a fact, but when Bruce began to hoot, she was sorry she'd said anything.

"You sing in the *choir*?" Bruce asked Lowell, then pretended to laugh so hard he could barely stand up. "Oh, man, I shoulda known. I bet you sing like a little parrot! You should be on the girls' team!"

Mike and Tommy stared at the ground, small smiles leaking out the corners of their mouths, while Lowell fixed his eyes on Juliet, his betrayer.

"Parrots don't sing," Juliet said. "They only talk."

Bruce stopped laughing. "What do *you* know? Birds sing."

"Yeah, but not parrots," Patsy said, backing Juliet up.

"Who cares?" Bruce bellowed. "Girls think they're so smart!"

"So, what time tomorrow?" Patsy asked again.

"Meet here at two o'clock," Bruce said. "You should all be done singing and praying and being good little boys and girls by that time."

They sullenly agreed to meet at two, and the girls, including Caroline and Mimi, walked back to Juliet's yard. The teams did not say good-bye to each other.

Annette fussed with her ponytail and fumed. "They'll never get to like us at this rate. Bruce makes it seem like we're all terrible."

Linda was particularly unhappy. "What if they choose something really hard that I can't even *do*?" she asked.

"It has to be something Lowell can do too," Juliet reminded her. "It's not going to be walking a tightrope or anything."

"This is the silliest thing I ever heard of," Mimi said. "If you just want to talk to boys, there are better ways to do it than having races with them."

"Like what?" Annette wanted to know.

"She doesn't know," Juliet said. "If they knew how to talk to boys, they wouldn't be here talking to us."

Caroline glared at her sister as the older two went back inside the house. "See if I do you a favor again, snotface."

Annette waved at them. "Bye! See you later!" Then she told Juliet, "Your sister has the most beautiful hair!"

The foursome parted ways soon after, all of them gloomy with defeat. Linda had a stitch in her side, so she called her mom to come pick up her and Annette. Patsy slunk off down the alley to "finish my dumb homework," and Juliet sat alone on the front step of Klostermeyer's Market, watching nervously as a military plane from Lathrop roared low over the neighborhood.

chapter eight

Over dinner that night Caroline tried to explain to their parents that Juliet was involved in a foolish, and possibly dangerous, contest against a group of boys, but they were too preoccupied by their own troubles to pay much attention.

"But Mom," Caroline said, "Bruce Wagner is one of the boys! You know how wild he is! I don't think Juliet should be allowed to keep doing this."

"I think it's nice the boys are including Bruce in their game," Ethel said. "That boy's alone too much. Lowell will be a good influence on him."

Caroline rolled her eyes. "If the police can't influence Bruce, I doubt that Lowell McManus can."

Juliet let her leg swing up into her sister's shin.

"Ow! She kicked me!"

"Stop it, you two," their father said. "I mean it. I have enough on my mind these days without having to listen to your silly arguments." He picked his well-done hamburger off the plate and stared at it through his bifocals, kneading the bun with his long thin fingers as if he were hesitant to bite into it.

"Eat your food before it gets cold," their mother told the girls. Her hair had outgrown its permanent, and she looked bedraggled. All that was left of the red lipstick she applied every morning and again after lunch was a thin, crusty outline that Juliet thought made her seem worn-out, faded.

"The peas are already cold," Juliet said, letting her fork smash the canned vegetables into mush.

"Be glad you have food on your plate!" their father said, much too loudly. "If we didn't own this store, the money I make wouldn't be enough to buy us groceries!" He plopped the burger back down onto his plate.

"Don," Ethel said, "don't get yourself all upset. Eat your dinner."

"You know as well as I do that we make our week on Saturdays—and we sure didn't make it today. If our regular customers are deserting us and shopping at those damn supermarkets, we aren't going to survive! That's the God's truth!"

"Don't swear in front of the girls," Ethel said. She always said that, even though the girls had been raised on a steady diet of her husband's strong language. "We've made it this far; we'll—"

"No, Ethel, we won't! The Mattesons still come, but where were the Heinnemans today? And Mrs. Fleck? And the Shullenbergers haven't been here in months. We can't afford to lose anybody else."

"We've got some new customers too. What about the Osgoods—Patsy's family?"

"Sure, sure, a few new people come. But they don't buy like the Heinnemans or some of our old customers. They don't have the money."

"Patsy's family doesn't have enough money?" Juliet asked.

"Now see?" Ethel said, her eyes imploring her husband to be quiet. "No more talk about this at the dinner table."

"We're the ones that don't have enough money," Caroline told Juliet. She picked the onion slice off her hamburger and set it aside. "Which I suppose means I won't get that skirt and sweater set for my birthday that I saw at the Carroll House."

"Your birthday is a month away. We'll discuss it later," Ethel said.

But Caroline couldn't let it go. "Mimi got a new outfit for her birthday, and a transistor radio, too. It isn't fair."

Dad brought his fist down on the table so hard that the silverware jumped at the same time his family did. "Life isn't fair! And you're not Mimi! And speaking of Mimi, what the hell happened to *her* parents? Did the Ebersoles just disappear from the face of the earth? They sure don't shop here anymore!"

"Don!" Ethel said, but he was not to be stopped.

"If I ever hear that either of you girls set foot in a supermarket, I will paddle your behinds—I don't care how old you are! Those damn stores are putting us out of business, and you are *never* to go inside one! Do you understand me?"

Juliet and Caroline nodded, and a tear rolled down Caroline's cheek. She hated for anyone to raise their voice to her. Juliet didn't like it either, but she prided herself on being tougher than her sister. When her father started to yell, Juliet could switch off the sound—or at least switch off her reaction to it. She could dig down inside herself to a place where the yelling didn't hurt so much.

"Go upstairs, girls. I want to talk to your father," Ethel said.

"I'm not finished eating yet," Juliet said.

"Take your plate with you, then!" Food was never allowed upstairs, but Juliet wasn't going to argue. She pushed back her chair, picked up her plate and carefully followed Caroline, who'd already run up to their room.

Caroline threw herself on her bed and dried her eyes with a corner of her pillowcase. "I hate when Daddy gets mad like that. It's like he's some awful person I don't even know."

"It seems like he's always mad these days." Juliet sat cross-legged on her bed, the plate balanced between her knees, and took a large, ketchup-soaked bite of her hamburger.

"You better not get ketchup on your bedspread," Caroline said. "Mom'll kill you."

"She told me I could bring it up here."

"Still."

"Are we really poor?" Juliet asked her sister.

"No. I don't know. Maybe we are."

They were silent for a minute, and then Juliet asked, "Have you ever gone into a supermarket?"

Caroline raised her eyebrows. "Are you kidding?"

"I mean just to see what they're like. Not to buy anything."

"Of course I haven't, and you better never go into one either. You saw how upset Dad gets just thinking about supermarkets. He would tan your hide for sure if he found out you actually went into one."

"I didn't say I was going to do it. I just wonder what they look like inside. It would be interesting to see. They're so big. What all is in them? I mean, we've got all the food you need in our store. What else could they have?"

Caroline kicked off her loafers. "Lots of stuff. Like twenty or thirty different kinds of cereals and cookies and soda. Tons of frozen stuff we don't have room for in our store."

"You said you never went in one!"

"I haven't. But Mimi's parents shop at the Kroger down on Route 47—Dad was right about that. You should see the stuff they buy."

Juliet was outraged. "How come they don't shop at our store anymore? She's your best friend!"

"Because, stupid, it's a lot cheaper to shop at super-markets. You can save money. And you have more choices, too."

Juliet wiped her greasy hands on her jeans. "I thought maybe the Ebersoles were mad at Dad or something. He's got a bad temper sometimes."

"He doesn't yell at the customers! God, Juliet, some-times you say the dumbest things." Caroline sighed, turned over onto her back, and stared at the ceiling.

Juliet stuck her tongue out at her sister—as far out as it would go—but Caroline had her eyes closed and didn't notice. The voices, which had been a low rumble in the background, escalated into a full-blown storm and came rolling up from downstairs.

"Oh, you blame everything on the president!" Ethel said.

"That's because he's a jackass!" Don shot back.

"John Kennedy didn't invent supermarkets, Don."

"He wants to waste our hard-earned tax money sending a man to the moon! What kind of nonsense is that? If he'd lower taxes, people could spend their *own* money—in our store! I'd like to send JFK to the moon."

"And sometimes I'd like to send you to the moon. Maybe you could be the first man to go!"

"Sign me up! Anything to get out of this rat race!" The sound of clattering dishes was followed by a crash.

"Oh, Don, now look what you did!" Ethel said. A door slammed.

Caroline pulled her pillow from under her head and placed it over her face so she couldn't hear anything else. Juliet leaned back against the headboard of her bed, determined to finish every last bite of her hamburger, but not another pea.

chapter nine

The Klostermeyers usually slept in on Sundays. It was the only day that Ethel and Don didn't have to get up early and open the store. They belonged to the First Presbyterian Church but seldom roused themselves to get dressed up and drive down there. Sometimes Caroline got up early enough to go to church with Mimi's family, and Juliet went with the McManuses once in a while, but that Sunday morning they were all too tired to bother. Juliet didn't really care about sitting in church anyway—the sermons were usually long and boring and never discussed the things she was worried about. You didn't need to sit in a church pew to talk to God.

While Caroline was in the bathroom, Juliet took advantage of being alone in their room to send another quick prayer out into the atmosphere.

God, you ought to know that a lot of things aren't very fair. One is that some people have a lot of money and other people don't have much, even though they work hard. If you could figure out a way for everybody to have enough money, people probably wouldn't fight so much. And also, please don't forget to keep an eye on the Russians to make sure they don't bomb us. I've asked you that before, but it's important, so I figured a reminder wouldn't hurt.

"I couldn't get to sleep last night," Caroline complained as they came downstairs for a late breakfast. "They were up arguing till all hours. You didn't have any problem, though. You were snoring by nine o'clock."

"I was not snoring." Juliet socked her sister on the arm. "Could you please stop insulting me for five minutes, Caroline? That's all you ever do!"

"Could you please stop hitting me all the time?"

"Girls!" Ethel barked at them. "I cannot stand another argument this morning!"

She stood at the stove pouring pancake batter into an iron skillet, but their father, Juliet could see, was drinking coffee in the living room by himself, the *St. Louis Post-Dispatch* held up over his face.

"Pour yourselves some milk," Ethel directed as she flipped the pancakes.

Caroline got the bottle out of the refrigerator and started to pour milk into two tumblers.

"I want my cup," Juliet said, and went to look for it in the dish drainer.

"Oh, Juliet." Ethel raised her hand, spatula and all, to her forehead and rubbed it hard. "I'm sorry. Last night when Dad and I were clearing the table, it got broken."

Juliet stared at her mother, stunned.

"When you and Dad were arguing, you mean?" Caroline asked.

Ethel sighed. "*Yes*, when we were arguing."

"It was an accident," Dad yelled in from the other room. "It was standing too close to the edge of the counter. I barely touched it."

"But that was Grandpa's cup!" Juliet said.

"I know, Juliet," her mom said. "I'm sorry."

Dad rattled the newspapers. "It was just a cheap cup from the racetrack. It's not like I killed your puppy. Let's not make a federal case out of this, shall we? Eat your breakfast."

Ethel reached out and put her hand on Juliet's arm. "Dad's sorry," she whispered, unconvincingly.

Juliet could tell by her father's tone of voice and her mother's apology (which sounded more like a warning) that any further complaint from her would result in Don's barely tamped-down anger flaring up again. She swallowed three or four times to push the sadness back inside so it wouldn't leak out into her voice.

"Where is it?" she asked.

"I threw it away," Ethel said, motioning to the garbage pail. "It's in too many pieces to be glued."

Juliet lifted the lid on the can and pushed aside some eggshells and a bread wrapper so she could get to the familiar ivory china. Four large pieces and lots of smaller ones littered the trash. She picked out the large ones and held them in her hand. The head of the racehorse was on one piece and the rest of him on another, but at least she could still see him.

Caroline stood next to her. "Let's wash them off," she said, turning on the hot water faucet. "You can keep them wrapped in a handkerchief."

Juliet nodded, surprised that Caroline understood the cup's importance to her. Understood better than her mother, who should have known better than to throw the cup away, no matter how many pieces it was in.

"Pancakes are done," Ethel said, as she distributed them among three plates. "You sure you don't want any, Don?"

"I have no appetite," he said curtly, angrily, as if, thought Juliet, *he* was the one whose favorite possession had been carelessly broken.

After choking down a pancake Juliet ran upstairs to put the pieces of the cup in her best handkerchief. She put the bundle in the corner of the drawer in her night table, where she could look at it before bed if she wanted to. At least the cup would be with her all the time now—her parents couldn't harm it any more than they already had.

She tried to focus on her homework, a dozen math problems to solve and twenty pages of geography to read. In case Mom or Dad was looking for trouble later on, she'd be able to say, yes, she'd finished all her homework and could watch *Ed Sullivan*. But concentrating on her homework was impossible. The image of Grandpa's racehorse cup, broken to pieces and thrown in the trash, haunted her, until finally she took the handkerchief full of china out of the drawer and held the pieces in her hand. *If I was Caroline,* she thought, *I'd be crying buckets.* Tears slid down the sides of her nose and dripped onto her sweater.

At one o'clock her mother made her a peanut butter and jelly sandwich, which Juliet pried open and lined with a layer of potato chips to cheer herself up. Then she called Patsy.

"You ready?" she asked.

"Absolutely! Today we win." Patsy sounded very sure of herself.

"Meet you in front of the store in five minutes."

Patsy and Juliet had half an hour to discuss strategy before the contest began, but since they didn't know what it was going to be, it was hard to prepare.

"It'll probably be some kind of game or sport thing," Patsy said. "They think we aren't as strong as they are."

"We *aren't* as strong as they are," Juliet reminded her. "We're as strong as Lowell—stronger—but we'll never beat Bruce at anything. Or Mike, either, probably."

"That's a lousy attitude! My dad always says to think positively. If you think you can do it, you *can* do it."

If that's true, wouldn't your dad be a pilot instead of a

mechanic? Juliet thought. But at least she didn't say it.

Mike and Tommy were dropped off by a woman in a big station wagon, and Lowell met them outside. In another minute Bruce came loping down the alley. His legs seemed longer and his feet bigger every time Juliet saw him.

"Where are those girls?" Patsy smacked her beat-up tennis shoe against the white siding of the storefront, and it left a black mark. "They better show up, that's all I have to say. If they chicken out, I'll kill 'em."

Just then a car pulled up, and Annette jumped out of the front seat, waving at them. Linda slowly crawled from the backseat.

"It's about time," Patsy said. "Let's get over there and hear what we have to do."

Linda groaned. "I hate this. I can't do this stuff."

Patsy turned around midstride and stuck her face right into Linda's. "I don't wanna hear the word 'can't' come out of your mouth. You can and you *will*."

Linda seemed shocked, but at least the ready-to-cry look vanished from her face. Juliet came up beside her and said, "Jeez, your old tennis shoes look better than my new ones." When Linda smiled halfheartedly, Juliet continued. "You don't have to win—you just have to try."

The girls marched over to Lowell's yard in a solemn line, Patsy in the lead, as usual. They were a dozen yards away from the boys when suddenly Bruce whipped his arm out from behind his back and leveled a baseball directly at Patsy's head. There was a collective intake of breath as the others saw the ball leave his hand.

"Think fast!" he yelled.

And Patsy did. Her hands came up and cupped the ball just before it would have smashed into her forehead.

"Mary and Joseph!" she yelled. "You just about beaned me with that thing! You're nutty as a fruitcake!"

Bruce bent double with laughter, and Patsy threw the ball back at him. It ricocheted off his shoulder and rolled into the grass. It must have hurt, but he didn't let on. "Oh, man, you shoulda seen the look on your face!"

"What's wrong with you? You could have really hurt her," Juliet said.

"You're lucky she caught it," Mike said. "That wasn't the smartest thing to do."

Bruce stopped laughing and glared at Mike. "What are you, sticking up for the girls now? She caught it, didn't she?"

"I'm just saying, a baseball is heavy. You could hurt somebody."

Before she thought too much about it, Juliet said, "Why do you even want to hang out with any of us, Bruce? You treat everybody terrible! You're not even nice to the boys!" It was the first time in her life Juliet had spoken up to Bruce Wagner, and her voice was trembling, but she really wanted to know the answer.

Bruce glared at her in silence for what felt like five minutes but was probably only seconds. Then he sputtered, "What am I supposed to do? There's nobody else for me to hang around with in this boring neighborhood."

And then Juliet got it: Bruce Wagner didn't have any friends. Of course he didn't. Nobody liked him, and the kids from his original grade had already moved on to the junior high school. These boys didn't like him either, but they were two years younger and at least a little bit afraid of him. Who wouldn't be? Bruce must have just shown up one day, and they didn't know how to get rid of him.

"Okay, okay," Patsy said. "Let's get this show on the road. What are we doing this time?"

"It's nothing too hard," Tommy said. "Don't worry."

"Not hard for *us*, anyway," Bruce said. He picked up the baseball and a bat that had been leaning against the house. "Just a simple game of who-can-hit-the-ball-the-farthest."

Linda groaned again, and Patsy gave her the evil eye.

"Scoring is the same as last time. You get points for winning and coming in second, third, fourth, and fifth." Bruce began walking toward Grove Street, and the others followed him. "You throw the ball up yourself–so you can't blame the pitcher–and hit it straight down the street. We mark the first place it hits. One boy and one girl judge, so it's fair."

Lowell had brought chalk again, so he marked a line for the batter to stand behind.

"Ladies first," Bruce said, and handed the bat to Lowell.

"He's on your team," Juliet said. "You aren't supposed to be mean to people on your own team." When Lowell leveled a nasty look in her direction, she added, "Not that I care. In fact maybe you aren't mean enough to him. Remember when we were in second grade and you used to call him Lowell the Mole?"

"Shut up, Juliet!" Lowell said, then mumbled, "I'll go first and get it over with."

Juliet knew Lowell was no better at hitting a baseball than he was at running. He was kind of a klutzy kid. But he had his mouth screwed up in determination now, and, though she didn't want to, Juliet couldn't stop herself from hoping he'd somehow manage to hit the ball.

He threw it up, swung the bat, and missed.

"God Almighty, you *are* a girl!" Bruce said. "You can't even hit a baseball!"

"Hey, jerkface, girls can hit baseballs—you just wait and see!" Patsy said.

Nobody else said a word. Juliet had the feeling that even the other girls were pulling for Lowell now.

He threw the ball in the air again, and as it came down, he swung at it hard—and it connected. The sound of the ball thwacking off the wooden bat pleased Juliet so much she jumped in the air; then she caught herself and settled down before anyone noticed. The ball didn't go straight, but it went for a decent distance, finally banging into the curb and rolling away.

Mike had the chalk and he conferred with Annette as to exactly where to make the mark. Annette was thrilled.

Patsy got the bat next and banged the ball far down the street, whooping at her own skill. Tommy had a good hit too, but not as far as Patsy's. Linda was afraid of the ball and only managed to bunt it a few yards, after which she scowled at Patsy and said, "I *told* you."

Bruce was up next. He cracked his knuckles, wiped his hands on his pants, and circled the bat in the air like he was batting for the Cardinals instead of just hitting balls down Grove Street. Finally, he threw the ball in the air and smacked it a good one when it came down. It flew and flew and flew. And landed just past Patsy's.

When Mike and Annette reported the news, Bruce hollered, and Patsy ran the length of the block to make sure they'd gotten it right. "Two lousy inches!" she said as she stomped away.

Juliet's hit was not her best, but the ball went a little past where Lowell's had. She almost wished it hadn't. Then Mike and Annette—the final contenders—came from the outfield to bat.

Mike went first, smashing it a good one. His ball sailed far into the air and came down a foot or so shy of Patsy's. She rejoiced.

"Okay, Annette," she said. "It's up to you. Can you hit the darn ball at all? You're our last chance!"

"I'm not bad," Annette said. "Just get out of my way." And then she proceeded to smack the ball hard. It followed almost the same trajectory that Mike's had, and when it hit the pavement, Juliet, now out in the field, couldn't believe it. "It hit right where Mike's hit!"

Tommy agreed. "Exactly the same spot. Strange, huh?"

"Wow, that was boss. Who taught you to play baseball?" Patsy asked her.

Annette was beaming. "My older brother. I told you I wasn't bad. You think just because I comb my hair and tuck in my blouse I can't do any sports stuff, but I can."

It was decided that Mike and Annette had both come in third and should both receive three points. Patsy tallied the results quickly, but she wasn't pleased. Bruce had won and Patsy had been second, just as before. Mike and Annette had tied for third, and Tommy had been fifth. The final score was nine to seven in favor of the boys.

"At least we did better this time," Annette said. "We only lost by two points."

"So what? Losing is losing," Patsy said as she banged her fist against her leg.

"Yes, it is!" Bruce agreed. "We're two for two. And since we won, we get to pick the test again tomorrow. Unless you're ready to give up and admit you can't do it."

"We're not admitting anything, you germ," Patsy said.

"Tomorrow, after school, three o'clock," Bruce said. "We'll make it three for three."

"I doubt that," Patsy said.

"I don't," Linda mumbled. Patsy shoved her elbow into Linda's side.

"Okay, let's go to the go-kart track," Bruce said to the guys. Juliet couldn't help but notice that the other three exchanged exasperated glances. *At least,* she thought, *we don't have to spend the rest of the day with him.*

chapter ten

Since Caroline was out, the girls spent the rest of the afternoon brooding in Juliet's room. At least, Patsy brooded; Juliet tended to be more of a worrier and Linda a complainer.

Annette was still glowing from her fine performance with a baseball bat. "Isn't it funny the way my ball hit at exactly the same place Mike's did?" she said. "I think that means something, don't you? Maybe we're meant to be together!"

"My shoulder hurts," Linda said, rubbing it.

Juliet wished it wasn't rude to read when you had guests over. Looking at *Mad* magazine would make her forget about the afternoon's defeat. When Juliet had imagined having the room to herself and her friends, she'd pictured them having fun, not moping over some stupid contest.

"You know what we should do?" Patsy said. "We should pick our test now, so we can practice it ahead of time. Then when we win, we'll be ready. We'll have an edge on them."

The others looked at Patsy doubtfully. "*When* we win?"

Linda said. "Do you really think we're ever going to win against them?"

Patsy leaped off the bed and towered over Linda, who was sitting on the rug on the floor. "Not with an attitude like yours, we won't! Haven't you ever heard of positive thinking?"

"It's not my thinking ability I'm worried about," Linda said. "I'm not good at this sports stuff!"

"Wait a minute!" Juliet had an inspiration. "That's it! Linda should come up with our test! It should be something she can do and boys can't."

Patsy perked up. "Hey, that's not a bad idea."

"Like what?" Linda wasn't convinced. "Washing dishes? My mom says my dad can't do that worth beans."

"No! It has to be something that's a test of strength or skill or something like that," Patsy said.

Annette had been sitting in front of Caroline's dressing table, dabbing on little bits of makeup and squirts of perfume, but suddenly she turned around. "I know! Dancing! Linda is a great dancer, and I'm pretty good too. We could do the Twist—I'm sure the boys won't be able to do that!"

Linda stopped slouching. "That's a great idea. Who would judge us, though?"

"Wait, wait, wait," Patsy interrupted. "Dancing is a girl thing. It has to be something hard, so we can prove to them that we're as good as they are."

"That's dumb," Annette shot back. "Why shouldn't they have to prove they're as good as *we* are? Besides, dancing is as hard as a sport."

"Yeah," Linda said.

Patsy looked at Juliet.

"I think they're right," Juliet said. "And the boys would never be able to do it. Of course, I can't do it either."

"Me neither," Patsy admitted.

Linda jumped to her feet, full of enthusiasm now. "We'll teach you! Like you said, we can practice ahead of time. Oh, come on, Patsy, this'll be a blast!"

By the time Caroline came home, Chubby Checker was on the record player, and the four girls were bending their knees, rotating their hips, and laughing like crazy— even Patsy.

"What's going on in here?" Caroline said. "Are you playing my records?"

"Just this one," Juliet said, then explained why.

"You're still doing that challenge thing?"

"We have to," Patsy said. "It's not right for boys to think they're better than us."

"Yeah," Juliet said. "Lowell thinks I'm not good enough to hang around with him anymore. I wanna show him."

Caroline sighed. "Okay, okay. I can help you if you want. Annette and Linda have it down, but you two look like wet noodles. Don't let your arms flop around like that.

You have to rotate on the balls of your feet." She grabbed her sister's waist and showed her how to move her hips one direction and the top of her body the other. Just like Chubby.

So the girls were ready with their test, but they had to win one of the boys' tests first. Monday afternoon they met again at Lowell's. The wind had picked up, and Linda's mother had made her wear a scarf and hat, though Juliet thought that was going to extremes—she believed a hat should never be worn before Thanksgiving and a scarf was only necessary if you were traveling to Alaska by dogsled.

Bruce stood with his hands on his hips, smirking as usual.

"You better not throw anything at me," Patsy said, approaching cautiously.

He held his hands out to prove they were empty. "Today's test is a different kind," he said. "It's about who's the bravest."

"How come you always get to tell us about the test?" Patsy asked. "Let somebody else do it this time."

Bruce scowled, but he turned to the other boys. "Anybody want to?"

"I will," Mike said. "There's this dog that lives up the alley—"

"Mrs. Shepard's dog," Bruce said.

"You mean that big lug that barks its brains out every time I walk past?" Patsy asked.

"Yeah. He's big and scary. Whoever has the nerve to climb over the fence and get into the yard with the dog, their team wins."

"So, we don't all have to do it?" Linda asked.

"No. Anybody who wants to can do it, but you don't have to," Mike clarified.

"Anybody who's *brave* enough can do it," Bruce said.

Juliet was surprised; didn't Lowell remember that she used to play with Boneguard when he was a puppy? Not that she was anxious to get inside the fence with him these days, but she'd probably have an advantage over the rest of them. She tried to catch Lowell's eye, but he wouldn't look at her.

As they walked down the alley, the boys led the way. Patsy walked next to Juliet. "I'm not that crazy about dogs," she said. "I got bit by a mutt in Tucson. Twice, actually, by two different dogs."

"I might be able to do it," Juliet whispered back. "And anyway, Mrs. Shepard told me once that Boneguard doesn't like men. He'll never let the boys inside."

As they got closer to the fence, the dog came running, growling as he ran, then threw himself against the high fence as if it weren't even there.

"Dang," Tommy said. "That's the biggest dog I've ever seen! I'm not going in there!"

"One coward has spoken. Anybody else?" Bruce leaned his hand on the fence, and Boneguard went for it so fast that Bruce practically fell over getting out of the way.

Patsy laughed and the other girls snickered. Juliet could tell the boys wanted to laugh too, but they didn't dare.

"Man, that dog's mean." Bruce shook a fist at Boneguard. "I'll show you, you mangy fleabag!" He spit at the animal, but his spit fell into the dust of the alley.

"Yeah, that's a good way to get him to like you," Juliet said. "I'll tell you one thing: Nobody's going to get in there with all of us standing around. We have to do it one at a time. Everybody else should go"—she looked across the alley—"behind the car in Mr. Colson's garage so Boneguard can't see them."

"Girls are such know-it-alls," Bruce said. "Who's going first?"

Linda and Annette shook their heads. "There's no way I'm getting close to that animal," Linda said.

"And Tommy's out," Bruce said. "How about you, Lowell? Any chance you suddenly turned into Superman?"

Lowell shook his head.

"I'm *so* surprised."

Patsy hung her head. "Um, I guess I'm out too."

"What? The bigmouth isn't even gonna try?" Bruce said.

"I can't!" Patsy yelled. "I'm allergic to dog bites!"

"I never heard of such a thing. You're just chicken."

"I am not! You take that back!" The more Patsy yelled, the louder Boneguard barked.

Bruce turned away from Patsy. "Anybody else? How about you, Mike?"

Mike took a step closer to the fence. "Hey, fella," he said. "How ya doin'?" Boneguard leaped right for his face, and Mike fell back from the fence fast. "Forget it. Nobody can go in there. That dog's crazy."

"I'll do it," Juliet said, her heart pounding. "But the rest of you have to go hide like I said."

"Juliet, I don't think you ought to try this," Linda said.

"Positive thinking!" Patsy reminded them. "Maybe she can do it."

Everyone but Juliet went behind the car in the garage and ducked down so they couldn't be seen. Bruce peeked around one side of the car and Patsy peeked from the other so they could report what was happening.

"And don't come out until I'm on this side of the fence again," Juliet said. A quick prayer, she thought, couldn't hurt. *Dear God, please make Boneguard remember all those hot dogs I fed him when he was a puppy.*

From a distance she started to talk quietly to the dog. "Hey, Boney, remember me? I used to come and play with you when you were little. You liked it when I scratched you behind the ears."

At first the dog barked and growled, but the more she talked, the more Boneguard calmed down. His ears weren't laid back anymore, and his tail started to wag the slightest bit. Finally, Juliet dared to put out her hand, slowly, until it was on the top of the fence. Boneguard jumped up, and for a minute Juliet panicked, but the dog only licked her. She continued to talk quietly to him, then scratched him under the chin. It took her at least ten minutes to carefully insert her foot into the fence notch and swing herself over. Once she was inside, Boneguard was as sweet as she'd remembered him. He turned over onto his back and let her scratch his stomach; he licked her face and pushed his big head into her armpit, begging for more attention. Juliet realized the dog was probably lonely fenced up outside all day, and she vowed to come visit him more often.

When she climbed back across the fence, Boneguard whined.

"I'll come back and see you again," she promised him. Then she crossed to the garage.

"I can't believe you did that!" Tommy said.

"We win!" Patsy shouted, banging Juliet on the back; the other girls did the same. All the noise made Boneguard bark again.

"Not yet you don't," Bruce said. "I haven't had a chance. If I do it, we're tied."

He hitched up his blue jeans like some Wyoming cowboy, said, "I'm not afraida some stupid dog," and headed out of the garage.

"He'll never be able to do it," Lowell whispered. It sounded like he was glad.

"Hey, there, buddy!" Bruce said as he approached Boneguard. "How ya doin'? You gonna let me climb in there and rub your belly?"

The dog's ears were flattened against his skull, and though he'd stopped barking, the low growl could be heard across the alley. His eyes were focused on Bruce's face as if he was just waiting for the chance to sink his teeth into it.

But Bruce wasn't reading the signs. As he put his foot in the fence notch, Boneguard backed away from him.

"Don't be afraid of me, fella," Bruce said. "I'm your friend!" He grabbed two pickets with his hands and swung his left leg up and over the fence.

But the second Bruce's foot was inside Boneguard's yard, the dog leaped on it, making an awful snarling sound in his throat. The seven people in the garage stood up so they could see better, but none of them said a word.

"Ow! Ow! Let me go, you dumb dog!" Bruce kicked his foot around until Boneguard's grip loosened; then he fell back into the alley. "Mary and Joseph!" he yelled, and kicked at the fence with his undamaged foot. "You oughta be shot, you stupid mutt!"

As he pulled up his pants leg to check the damage, Mrs. Shepard came out through her back door. "What on earth is going on out here?" she said. "Bruce Wagner, are you tormenting my dog?"

"Me?" Bruce shouted. "Look what that animal did to me! He bit me!"

"Well, he wouldn't have bit ya unless you tried to come over the fence. Did you come over the fence?"

"I . . . I just wanted to pet him."

"Not a good idea, Bruce," she said, peering at his leg. "That don't look like a bite to me. You just ripped his pants up a little bit, didn't ya, Boney?" She patted the dog and he licked her hand.

"If I wasn't wearin' a shoe, he'd a took my foot off!"

"Let that be a lesson to ya. Don't go climbing over people's fences when you haven't been invited." She called to Boneguard, and he wagged his tail as he followed her into the house.

Patsy came dancing out from the garage. "We won! Fair and square! You have to do our test tomorrow!"

The others followed her into the alley, where Bruce stood staring at the Shepards' house and fuming.

"You call that fair? That dog is nuts!"

"I did it," Juliet reminded him. "You just have to know

how." She was really beginning to enjoy making Bruce angry, especially when Patsy was around to back her up.

"They won," Mike said. "You can't argue with that. Juliet was the only person to make it over the fence."

"Yeah, there was something fishy about that," Bruce said. "Did you have a dog biscuit in your pocket or something?"

"Why would I have a dog biscuit? I don't even have a dog. Besides, I didn't know what your test was going to be, did I?"

Bruce grumbled as he limped away up the alley. "I'm goin' home."

"Wait a minute," Patsy called after him. "Tomorrow's test is at Linda's house after school."

"At 202 High Street," Linda said. "Around the corner from Jefferson. My mom will be the judge."

Bruce didn't look pleased about the change of venue. "What's the test?" he wanted to know.

"You'll find out tomorrow," she said.

Bruce made a face at her, but his heart wasn't in it. He shuffled home.

The rest of them walked back toward Juliet and Lowell's end of the alley.

"That was amazing, Juliet," Annette said. "I would never have gone into that dog's yard."

"Yeah, me either," Mike said. "You deserved to win this one."

"Hey," Tommy said. "Why did the elephant cross the road?"

"Why?" Patsy asked.

"Because it was the chicken's day off!"

They all laughed a giddy, relieved laugh. Another test was over, and Bruce had gone away.

chapter eleven

Juliet hurried through her homework so she could watch television after dinner, first *Mister Ed* and then *The Beverly Hillbillies*. As her mother washed the dishes, Juliet dried them, throwing the silverware into the drawer noisily and banging the pots down on top of the stove.

"Is there a race I'm not aware of?" her mother asked.

"I want to watch *Mister Ed*," Juliet said. "It starts in five minutes."

"That is the dumbest program," said Caroline, who was sitting at the kitchen table making a long chain out of folded gum wrappers. "Who ever heard of a talking horse?"

"That's why it's *funny*," Juliet shot back. "If you had brains, you'd be dangerous."

Ethel sighed. "I think I'll watch with you. I missed the news tonight, and I need to sit down and relax for a few minutes before I start the bookkeeping."

"Good!" Juliet stuck the wet dish towel through the handle of the refrigerator door and raced into the living room. Her mother seldom had time to sit with her for any reason, so Juliet looked forward to snuggling next to her on the couch for half an hour. Ethel had never been one for having chatty conversations with her girls, but she was always happy to let them sit on her lap or nestle in next to her.

But at seven o'clock, when *Mister Ed* was supposed to come on, something strange happened. First a sign appeared on the screen that said SPECIAL BULLETIN, and then the Channel Five news anchor came on the air and said, "Instead of our regularly scheduled broadcast, we will now bring you a special report from the president of the United States."

"What?" Juliet said. "Where's *Mister Ed*?"

"Oh, no," her mother said. "This can't be good."

In another minute President Kennedy was on the air, looking handsome as always, but not smiling. "Good evening, my fellow citizens," he began, his voice sounding terribly serious.

"Don!" Ethel called. "Come in here! Something's happened! Hurry!"

Don had been in the store, preparing the meat counter for the morning, so Caroline arrived before he did. They both came in asking questions, but Ethel shushed them so they could hear.

"This government, as promised, has maintained the closest surveillance of the Soviet military buildup on the island of Cuba. Within the past week, unmistakable evidence has established the fact that a series of offensive missile sites is now in preparation on that imprisoned island. The purpose of these bases can be none other than to provide a nuclear strike capability against the Western Hemisphere."

"What does that mean?" Caroline said. Her voice was squeaky, and she was already on the verge of tears. "Are we at war?"

"No, not yet," Ethel said. "Just listen."

"It's that Khrushchev!" Don said, banging his fist on the coffee table. "He wants to take over the world!"

Kennedy continued talking about the missile sites in Cuba:

"Several of them include medium-range ballistic missiles, capable of carrying a nuclear warhead for a distance of more than one thousand nautical miles. Each of these missiles, in short, is capable of striking Washington DC, the Panama Canal, Cape Canaveral, Mexico City, or any other city in the southeastern part of the United States, in Central America, or in the Caribbean area.

"Additional sites not yet completed appear to be designed for intermediate-range ballistic missiles, capable of traveling more than twice as far, and thus capable of striking most of the major cities in the Western Hemisphere, ranging as far north as Hudson Bay, Canada, and as far south as Lima, Peru. In addition jet bombers, capable of carrying nuclear weapons, are now being uncrated and assembled in Cuba, while the necessary air bases are being prepared."

"As far north as Canada!" Caroline began to cry and threw herself on her mother's neck. "It *is* war! They're going to kill us all!"

President Kennedy kept on talking while Don raged and Ethel consoled Caroline as best she could. Juliet, meanwhile, closed her ears the same way she did when her father was yelling. She just stopped listening to horrible things she couldn't bear to hear.

Still, she didn't think she'd ever been more frightened. She'd always cringed when people talked about war or bombs. And when her grandfather died, she'd started to imagine how frightening the future would be without her parents. But that had all been playing at fear, tempting it, testing it. This was real. Russia was building missiles that could blow up the whole world.

The president outlined the things the U.S. was doing to combat the danger: quarantine, surveillance, evacuation, every word more frightening than the one before. When Juliet heard him say the U.S. was willing, if need be, to launch a full retaliatory response, she understood that it meant not just a war but *the* war, the end of everything she knew. Could her nightmares really be coming true?

"My fellow citizens: Let no one doubt that this is a

difficult and dangerous effort on which we have set out. No one can foresee precisely what course it will take or what costs or casualties will be incurred. Many months of sacrifice and self-discipline lie ahead—months in which both our patience and our will will be tested—months in which many threats and denunciations will keep us aware of our dangers. But the greatest danger of all would be to do nothing."

Was that true? Juliet wondered. What if they just gave in and let the Soviet Union do what they wanted? They'd still be alive, wouldn't they? Or would Nikita Khrushchev kill them all, one by one? No, he wouldn't do that—he wanted to rule over them. *Well, let him,* she thought. *It's better than blowing up the whole world!*

Kennedy talked through most of *Mister Ed*'s half hour, and he was followed by the local newscaster's comments, but Don turned the set off.

"I can't take any more of this rubbish," he said. "We should have put the Russians in their place years ago. Kennedy has been too easy on them, and now look."

"Well, when you're elected president, I'm sure you'll do a better job," Ethel said, but her jab didn't have its usual sharpness.

Juliet had her legs tucked underneath her and her arms wrapped around her chest; she hadn't moved through the whole speech. "I wanted to watch *Mister Ed* with Mom," she said, and then the tears began to trickle down her cheeks. It suddenly seemed as if President Kennedy and the Russians and the newscasters had all stolen something precious from her that she could never get back.

Caroline was incredulous. "Oh my God, you're crying about a TV show? We're all going to be blown up, and you're upset because you couldn't watch a talking horse?"

Juliet unwrapped herself and stood up. "Go jump in a lake!" she yelled at her sister, and then ran upstairs before the crying could begin in earnest.

Juliet couldn't get to sleep that night, and she was pretty sure Caroline couldn't either. The two of them tossed and turned but didn't speak to each other. In fact the whole family looked bleary-eyed at the breakfast table, but when Patsy arrived, she was in much higher spirits than anyone in the Klostermeyer household.

"My dad says we got nothing to worry about," she said as they pedaled to school. "Our air force can bomb the heck out of Cuba before they shoot off even one missile. They got enough B-52s at Lathrop alone to stop those Commies."

Juliet wasn't convinced. "Then how come the president sounded so worried on television last night?"

"He has to sound that way. He doesn't want Russia to know we're planning a sneak attack!"

"That's not the way it sounded to me," Juliet said.

"I'm telling you, my dad knows all about this stuff, and he's not worried."

Juliet wondered if a mechanic would be likely to know about all the secret goings-on at an air base. Maybe Patsy's dad just wanted her to think he wasn't worried, so she didn't get scared.

"Does your dad talk to you a lot?" Juliet asked.

"Sure. He tells me everything," she said. But then, hopping off her bike at school, she added, "I mean, he's pretty busy these days, so I don't see him as much as I used to. And then there's David, too. He's always getting in the way and ruining things. You're lucky that your dad is around all day. You can see him whenever you want to."

Juliet had never thought having her father around was lucky. In fact she usually wished he was one of those fathers who drove off to a job in the morning and didn't come back until dinnertime. Especially if it was a job where he earned a lot of money and her mother could stay home and do mother-type stuff instead of working too. Her dad hardly ever talked to Juliet anyway—some days he hardly even *looked* at her—so what difference did it make that he was in the same building she was?

Mrs. Funkhauser started the school day off with a duck-and-cover drill, which she said was to reassure the students that they were well prepared in case an attack did occur.

Juliet curled into a ball under her desk and put her hands over her head like she was supposed to, but she couldn't help thinking that a desk wasn't much protection if a bomb hit your school.

Some of the kids were obviously taking this drill more seriously than earlier ones; Juliet saw a tear roll down the cheek of Annie Cole, who sat next to her. Patsy, of course, was hardly even bent over. She used the opportunity to sneak a stick of gum from her pocket and fold it quietly into her mouth.

Instead of continuing their discussion of Brazil in geography, Mrs. Funkhauser said she thought they should talk about Cuba today, so they would have some idea of where it was and who lived there. She pulled down the big map in the front of the room and pointed out a small island that looked pretty close to Florida. Too close. But also awfully small to be such a dangerous place.

Cuba was about the same size as Pennsylvania, Mrs. Funkhauser said, and only ninety miles from Key West, Florida. The people who lived there now were mostly the descendants of Spanish landowners and the African slaves who'd been brought there to work the sugar plantations. The agricultural products of the country were sugar, tobacco, citrus fruits, and coffee.

"The president of Cuba," she continued, "is Fidel Castro. He is a Communist devil who is controlled by

Russia. But you don't need to be afraid of him, because America is standing up to these bullies."

Annie Cole raised her hand. "I heard my mother say the Russians have bombs that can reach all the way here. She says Lathrop Air Field is number three on the list of places that will be bombed, and we'll all be killed."

"Oh, dear, I think your mother is letting her imagination run away with her. You tell her that we should be *happy* to live so close to Lathrop. That air base will be our protection against the bombs. I'm not worried, and I don't think you should be either."

Juliet tried to look deep into Mrs. Funkhauser's eyes to see if she was telling the truth about not being worried. But it was hard to tell with teachers. They all looked like they had varnish over their faces—it was hard to see if there were any cracks underneath the shine.

Finally, the long day was over. Patsy and Juliet met up with Linda and Annette and rode over to Linda's house.

"My dad is a civil defense warden," Linda said. "He had to go to emergency meetings all day today."

"What do you think they talk about in their meetings?" Annette asked. "How to save people's lives if a bomb hits?"

Linda shrugged. "I guess. I think most of the wardens have their own bomb shelters at home, though."

"Do you?" Patsy asked.

"Sure. We've had one for ages."

"Can we see it?"

"I've already seen it," Annette said, "but I don't think Juliet has, have you?"

Juliet shook her head. She wasn't sure she wanted to see it, but the boys hadn't arrived yet and there was nothing else to do, so she followed Linda and the others into the garage.

"It's underneath here," Linda explained as she led them inside. "Help me get the hatch open." The four of them tugged at a handle that eventually opened a flat, steel door into the ground.

"Be careful going down the ladder," Annette warned. "It's steep."

Patsy flew down the steps and leaped off at the bottom. "Wow! This is boss! There are beds down here and everything!"

"Well, sure, you have to have beds," Linda said. "You might have to stay here for a month or so until all the fallout is gone."

Juliet backed carefully down the ladder. The room wasn't much larger than her bedroom at home, only instead of single beds there were two sets of bunk beds, and shelves along the other walls. A small table and chairs took up the middle of the room, leaving barely enough room for all four girls to stand up.

"If I had to stay in a room this small with my parents and Robby for a month, I'd go crazy," Annette said.

"Yeah, but at least you wouldn't be dead," Patsy said. "I wish we had one of these."

"I thought you said there was nothing to worry about," Juliet reminded her. "You said your dad wasn't worried."

"He isn't. But it would still be cool to have a place like this. You could even play down here!"

Linda shook her head. "My dad never lets us play down here. If he was home, I wouldn't even bring you down. He's afraid we'll break something or eat something. He's got just enough supplies to last us for six weeks. There's even a medical kit and an air pump," she said proudly.

"Tell 'em what this is," Annette said, pointing to a big metal drum with the words SANITATION KIT lettered on the side.

"Um, that's sort of a toilet," Linda said.

"Can you imagine?" Annette said. "You'd have to go to the bathroom right out here in front of everybody! And it would smell!"

"There are chemicals inside so it doesn't smell," Linda explained. "I know it's kind of awful, but you need to have someplace to go! That big drum under the table is clean water."

"And this is all food?" Patsy asked, looking at shelves containing tin cans and boxes. "Most of these say 'survival crackers.'"

"They're specially made crackers that give you more vitamins and stuff than regular crackers."

"So you have to live on crackers and water for six weeks? That's like prison."

"I'd probably be too scared to eat anyway," Annette said.

Juliet's stomach was flipping over just imagining being shut up in this room for six weeks while bombs went off outside. She was sure she wouldn't be able to last a single day. And then she heard the voices overhead. She turned and put one foot on the lower rung of the ladder. "Hey . . . ," she said.

But it was already too late. The hatch banged shut.

chapter twelve

"We're locked in!" Juliet shouted, hoping the panic she was feeling wasn't completely obvious in her voice. "It was those darn boys!"

"How did they even know we were down here?" Annette said, a note of excitement creeping into her voice.

"They probably heard us talking. Good thing we've got all these crackers," Patsy said with a laugh.

"It's not locked," Linda said. "But it's too heavy for us to open from inside. My dad can do it, but I can't."

"Let us out!" Juliet shouted, sweat beading up on her forehead.

"They can't hear you," Linda said. "The blast door is steel and reinforced concrete."

Juliet glared at Linda. This place didn't feel safe at all—it felt like it would collapse right in on her. She had to get out!

"We might as well sit down and wait," Patsy said, flopping on a low bunk. "They'll get tired of their stupid game in a few minutes."

Not soon enough for Juliet, though. She climbed the ladder and banged on the hatch door. "Let us out, you imbeciles!" she screamed.

"Don't have a cow, Juliet," Linda said. "They have to open it up sooner or later."

Juliet thought it had better be sooner or her heart would burst right out of her chest. She was just about to scream again when the hatch began to squeak open. She could hear the boys arguing.

"God Almighty, they were only down there two seconds," Bruce said. "They ain't gonna die that fast. You guys are such chickens."

"We came here to do the test and then go home," Mike said. "Not to lock people in the ground."

"Who's talking about people?" Bruce said. "These are girls!"

Juliet scampered up the ladder the moment the hatch was open. "That wasn't funny!" she screamed in Lowell's face.

"It wasn't *my* idea!" he said.

"Gee," Patsy said as she emerged from the ground, "I wonder whose idea it was? Some real genius, I bet."

"Thanks for opening the hatch, Mike," Annette said, giving him a toothy smile.

Juliet realized the other girls weren't upset by Bruce's trick. She was the only one who'd been terrified down there.

She took a deep breath and tried to calm down. What did she think was going to happen anyway? That they'd be down there forever? It was the idea of being locked in a bomb shelter that had been so bad, she decided. As if it meant they *needed* to be there.

Linda led the way into the house. "My mom is going to be the judge," she said. "But don't worry. She won't play favorites."

"She *better* not," Bruce said, as though he'd be just as willing to beat up Linda's mother as anybody else. "What kind of test can you do in the house, anyway?"

"Dancing!" Annette announced. "We're going to have a Twist contest."

"Dancing?" Tommy said. "That's not the right kind of test."

"No way!" Bruce said. "I'm not dancing. That's for girls."

"It's a test of skill," Patsy said. "It's just as hard as hitting a baseball. Besides, it's our turn to choose, and we choose dancing."

The boys grumbled and complained, but they followed Linda into the dining room, where the furniture had already been pushed aside so they could twist on the hardwood floor.

Linda's mother looked a little harried when she came in, but she was nice to everyone. "Would you like a glass of lemonade before you start?" she asked.

Lowell said he would, but Bruce said, "No, let's just get this over with."

"Does anybody want any Twist lessons before we start?" Annette offered.

"No!" Patsy gave Annette a dirty look. "They didn't give us running lessons—we don't have to give them dancing lessons."

"I'm not dancing," Bruce said as he paced in the doorway. "This is stupid."

"Your funeral," Patsy said, smirking.

Linda had her record player set up in the corner of the room. She put the 45 on the turntable and set the needle on the record. Chubby Checker began to sing, inviting them, in his satiny voice, to "twist, baby, twist."

Linda and Annette started dancing immediately, while the boys watched them. Mike seemed to be hypnotized by Annette's waving ponytail and gyrating rear end.

"Somebody else better dance," Mrs. Wheeler said. "I'm supposed to rank the top five and I only have two!"

Patsy gave Juliet a punch on the arm, and the two of them self-consciously began to move their hips back and forth. It was embarrassing to do it in front of the boys. Juliet knew she and Patsy weren't really doing it right, but at least they were trying.

When she turned around, she was surprised to see that Lowell had started to dance too, and then Tommy and

Mike as well. The twins were just acting silly and throwing themselves around, but, surprisingly, Lowell actually seemed to know how the dance was done.

As she spun around on her pivoting toe, Juliet caught a glimpse of Bruce, arms out at his sides, attempting a subdued hip swivel. When he realized Juliet had seen him, he stopped moving and folded his arms over his chest, scowling.

"You all look spastic," he said.

"Look who's talking," Patsy shot back. "At least everybody else is a good sport."

Juliet wondered if Bruce might have eventually joined in the dancing if she'd pretended not to notice him trying out the steps. Sometimes she almost felt a little bit sorry for Bruce Wagner—until he said something to make her hate him again.

By the time the record wound down, the seven of them were dancing in a big circle and singing along, the boys making up the words they didn't know.

Tommy sang, "Come on, Clumsy, let's do the Twist. Even though we don't know how to, we're doing the Twist!" When the song ended, they fell to the floor, laughing.

Annette applauded. "That was fun! You guys did great!"

"It *was* kind of fun," Mike said.

"Should we do it again?" Annette asked, her eyes sparkly.

"No!" Bruce and Patsy said together.

"Who won?" Patsy asked Linda's mother.

"Well, let's see. It was hard to judge," she said tactfully. "But I guess I'd have to put Linda and Annette in the first two spots. They really know how to do the dance."

Nobody disagreed.

"And then I think this boy was the next best," Mrs. Wheeler said, pointing to Lowell, who blushed to his fingertips.

"What?" Patsy howled. "He was better than *me*?"

"Well, you and Juliet came in next," Mrs. Wheeler said. "As I said, it was hard to choose."

"Well, anyway," Patsy said, getting over the disgrace of being bested by Lowell pretty quickly, "the girls got four out of the top five spots, so we win!"

The girls cheered and the boys shrugged. All but Bruce. He pointed a finger at Patsy and said, "You think you're so smart picking a dance contest. But next time you better pick something everybody can do, or you'll be sorry."

Mrs. Wheeler had gone to get them lemonade, so she didn't hear the threat, but Juliet knew she probably wouldn't have done anything anyway. Adults never knew how to handle Bruce, so they mostly tried to ignore him.

"Don't you ever get tired of being in a bad mood all the time?" Juliet asked him.

But Bruce was too worked up to listen. "You know

what? This isn't just a challenge anymore. This means war! You hear me, guys? War!"

The dreaded word hit Juliet like a bolt of lightning, and her eyes sparked with fear. "It is not! We're not fighting—we're just testing ourselves."

"Maybe it started that way," Bruce said, "but you girls didn't play fair with this dancing thing—"

"We did too!" Patsy said, but Bruce talked right over her.

"And when you break the rules, the game turns into war! Just like what's happening with Russia. They got out of line, and we gotta push 'em back!"

The girls protested, but Bruce waved them away. "I'm leaving. I have better things to do than hang around with a bunch of idiot fifth graders."

"I doubt it!" Patsy called after him, but the rest of them were silent for a little while after that, contemplating the new battle cry.

Once they drained the lemonade pitcher, Annette had to get home for her piano lesson. The others were shocked when Mike offered to ride to her house with her.

"It's not that far," Juliet said. "It's only two blocks from here. She rides it by herself all the time."

Linda elbowed her and whispered, "Shut up!"

Tommy was surprised too. "Where should I go?" he asked Mike, as if making a decision without his twin brother had him baffled.

"Go home with Lowell. I'll come over there after," Mike called back to them. Annette's smile was lighting up her whole face.

Juliet, Patsy, Lowell, and Tommy pointed their bikes back to their neighborhood. Juliet had so many confusing thoughts racing through her mind that she would have sailed right through the stop sign at High Street and Lucinda Avenue, except that Lowell paused in front of her and reminded her to pay attention. They might have ridden in silence if Patsy hadn't been along, but silence was an unnatural condition for Patsy.

"What's with your brother going home with Annette?" she asked Tommy. "Does he like her or something?"

"I don't know," Tommy said.

"'Cause that's what it looked like to me," Patsy continued. "Like he wants to be her boyfriend or something. Which is against the rules of the challenge."

"I didn't know there was a rule like that," Lowell said.

"Well, we didn't *say* it, but that's always the rule. You can't be going out with somebody who's on the other team!"

"He isn't going out with her—he's just riding his bike to her house," Tommy said. "Hey, why do elephants have trunks?"

Nobody knew, so he supplied the answer. "Because they'd look silly with glove compartments!"

Patsy and Lowell laughed, but ever since the night before Juliet seemed to have lost her sense of humor.

"Oh, I know a good joke," Patsy said. "What do you call a cow with no legs?"

"What?"

"Ground beef!"

Pretty soon Patsy and Tommy were riding side by side, trading jokes. Lowell dropped back to ride with Juliet.

"Something wrong with you today?" he asked.

She shrugged. "No."

He was quiet for a minute, then said, "Is it about the Cuban stuff? The missiles and everything?"

"Sort of," she admitted. "It scares the heck out of me. I feel all jumpy, like it could happen any minute."

"Is that why you got so scared about being locked in the bomb shelter?"

She was still embarrassed about that, so instead of answering the question she just grunted.

"I'm sorry Bruce did that. I mean, I'm scared about the missile stuff too."

"Really?"

"Sure," Lowell said. "But don't tell Mike and Tommy. They say people who are afraid don't believe in the U.S. military. They think you're saying their father isn't brave or heroic or something."

"I don't think it's heroic to bomb people," Juliet said.

"Why is it supposed to be brave to kill people you don't even know?"

"That's not the way the twins see it."

"So, do you have to believe everything they believe now? Can't you even have your own opinions anymore?"

Lowell's face tightened. "Of course I can. I was trying to be nice to you, Juliet, but you just don't get it."

"I don't get boys, that's for sure!" she shouted at him. "And I don't want to."

"No skin off my nose!" Lowell yelled back. He picked up speed so he could join Patsy and Tommy in the lead.

Juliet rode half a block behind them and imagined a bomb falling to earth between them and her, disintegrating all the houses for miles around. She figured it probably wouldn't hurt. It would happen so fast you'd just disappear as though you'd never been there to begin with.

chapter thirteen

Before Lowell and Tommy left, Patsy announced that the next day's test would be tricks on roller skates. "So tell the other boys to bring their skates," she said. "Juliet, you call Linda and Annette."

"Shouldn't we ask them first if they want to do it?" Juliet said.

"They got to choose the dancing test. Besides, skating tricks are good," Patsy insisted. "It's something both girls and boys can do, so Bruce won't say we're cheating."

"Who'll judge?" Tommy asked.

Patsy brightened. "Maybe my dad can. And since I'm telling you now, we'll all have time to practice. How's that for fair?"

Juliet didn't want to practice skating. She wasn't in the mood. When Patsy went home, Juliet straggled inside to call the other girls.

Annette was too excited to take in what Juliet was saying. "Mike stood outside and talked to me for *fifteen minutes*! Can you believe it? I was late for my piano lesson, but who cares!"

"What did you talk about?" Juliet couldn't imagine talking to any boy that long. Except for Lowell, of course.

"I don't know. Just stuff."

"So, is he your boyfriend now?" Juliet asked.

"Maybe. I never had a boyfriend before!"

"Patsy won't like it," Juliet told her. "She says you can't go with anybody on the other team."

"Who made her the boss?" Annette said. "I don't have to do everything Patsy tells me to."

"I know," Juliet said, wishing she'd told Patsy to call the girls herself.

Talking to Linda was no fun either. "Do you think maybe Tommy will want to be *my* boyfriend?" she asked.

"I don't think Tommy's very interested in girls yet," Juliet said. *God, even if Khrushchev had missiles aimed directly at their houses, these two would still only want to talk about boys!*

"I know, but he likes to hang out with his brother, so if Mike is going with Annette and I'm Annette's best friend—"

"I have to go now," Juliet lied. "Don't forget to bring your skates tomorrow." She hung up and went to spend some time with Superman and Wonder Woman, who were able to escape even the most impossible situations.

Juliet's mother made sure they were finished with dinner in time to watch the news. Juliet didn't want to watch, but then she thought it might make her feel better. Maybe some solution had been found since the day before.

But all the newscasters looked just as solemn as they had last night. American ships were in the process of setting up a quarantine around Havana's harbor. No foreign ships carrying any kind of weapons or missile parts would be allowed through. She couldn't hear much else, because her parents started arguing.

"I can't believe that idiot Kennedy has gotten us into this mess," Don said. "Eisenhower would never have been so stupid!"

"Eisenhower was not a choice," Ethel reminded her husband. "It was JFK or that awful Nixon. And I certainly didn't trust him."

"Well, he couldn't have been much worse than this guy!"

"That's easy to say since we'll never know, will we?"

"Stop it! Stop it!" Caroline shrieked. "Who cares what the president did or didn't do? It's too late now anyway! At least you two got to grow up normally and get married and have children. You got to have your lives!" Tears beat down her cheeks, and she choked on them. "What about me? What about Juliet? We won't get to grow up or fall in love or anything! It's just not *fair*!"

Swiping at her face with the sleeve of her sweater Caroline ran from the room and could be heard sobbing all the way up the stairs.

"Now look what you did," Ethel said to Don.

"*Me?*" He shook his head in annoyance and headed back out to the store. Ethel switched off the television and followed Caroline, but not before turning to Juliet.

"Don't get scared," she said. "You know how overly dramatic your sister can be." Ethel's surface calm was betrayed by a nervous twitch in her eye.

Juliet wasn't sure you could be anything *but* overly dramatic when you were talking about the end of the world. Caroline wasn't making it up. Maybe she was right. Maybe they wouldn't grow up.

Dear God, I'd like to know if there's really a heaven, and if so, is it big enough for all the people who'd get killed by atomic bombs? Or would some of them have to go someplace else? If you die when you're still a kid, do you get to grow up in heaven or do you stay a kid forever? Being a kid is okay, but I don't want to be one for eternity. If heaven is such a great place, I think we should be able to grow up if we want to. I would at least like to be a teenager; otherwise Caroline will always be ahead of me. And, as my sister would say, that's just not fair!

In school they did duck-and-cover three times a day now—once in the cafeteria, which ruined Juliet's lunch. Nervous teachers had whispered conversations in the hallways. On the playground boys launched stick missiles at each other until Miss Newton made them stop. Juliet wanted desperately to get away from it all, but there was no place to go. The very air she breathed was filled with expectation and fear.

After school the girls rode their bikes to Klostermeyer's Market, where the sidewalk was long and smooth, unbroken by tree roots. They sat on the store step and tightened their skates with keys.

"I told my mom to come down at three thirty," Patsy said. "So we'd have a little time to practice first."

"I thought your dad was going to judge," Juliet said.

Patsy blew a large bubble with the Bazooka gum she'd just bought in the store, sucked it back into her mouth, and then said, "He can't. He's working overtime this week. He didn't even come home for supper last night."

That didn't sound so terrible to Juliet—suppertime without screaming—but she didn't say so.

Annette and Linda weren't half-bad skaters. They could do graceful turns and little jumps. Patsy specialized in racing full speed ahead down the sidewalk and leaping the curb into the side street, although once she almost ran into the side of a pickup truck, and the driver bawled the heck out of her. Juliet felt too tired to do tricks, but she half-heartedly lifted up her leg in back of her.

Bruce arrived, applauding and laughing. "Oh, wow, look at these daredevils skate!"

"Let's see what you can do!" Patsy yelled at him.

The boys had already put on their skates and were practicing high jumps. All but Bruce. He said he was "saving himself for the competition." Annette and Mike stood off to the side and talked for a few minutes, pretending not to notice Patsy's disgusted glare.

Patsy's mother arrived, with David holding onto her skirt and rolling along by her side in too-large skates.

"Why is he here?" Patsy demanded to know.

"Well, I couldn't very well leave him home alone, could I?" Her mother zipped up David's jacket and tousled his thicket of hair.

"Well, he can't get in our way," Patsy said. "This is a test!"

"I wanna skate too," David said.

Juliet held out her hand. "Here, I'll skate with you," she offered. Patsy treated her little brother so badly, Juliet sometimes felt she should make up for it.

"Not now, Juliet!" Patsy said. "We have to do the test first."

Juliet felt like yelling back at Patsy to stop bossing her around, but she didn't want Lowell to think they were having a fight. "When we're done, I'll skate with you," she promised David.

Patsy and Bruce wanted to go last so their superior skills would be appreciated in contrast to the others. But everybody was pretty good, even Lowell. They could all do simple jumps and turns and leg lifts. Nobody even tripped.

It was going to be hard to judge, Juliet thought.

Her turn came just before the final two. After seeing how well everyone else could skate, Juliet decided she'd better try something a little harder than she'd planned. She'd only managed this trick once before, but what did she have to lose? The idea was to get going fast, lift up one leg behind you and then hold it up as you bent down and almost touched the sidewalk. She sailed down the sidewalk, lifted her leg and leaned forward awkwardly, already tottering a little when David came running out from the grass.

"You said I could skate with you!" he cried, throwing himself at Juliet's hip. She tried to keep herself upright, but she only had one unsteady leg on the sidewalk to begin with. When that went out from under her, both of them toppled to the ground. David jumped up immediately, giggling, and ran off.

"David!" Patsy yelled. "Mom, I told you not to bring him!"

Mrs. Osgood ran to Juliet. "Are you okay?"

"I think so," Juliet said, but when Mrs. Osgood helped her up, she knew something was wrong. "Ow, my ankle really hurts."

"Oh no, I hope it's not broken. Lean on me."

"I don't think it's broken, but I can't skate anymore." The throbbing in her leg made Juliet wince.

"That's enough skating for today," Mrs. Osgood

announced to the group. "Let's get Juliet inside and—"

"Mom! We haven't finished the test yet! Juliet can sit on the grass for a few minutes until we're done."

"Patricia Marie, your friend is in pain!"

Juliet shook her head and limped to the lawn. "It's okay, Mrs. Osgood. I can wait until the test is over." Sure, her ankle hurt, but she didn't want to deal with Patsy's anger on top of it.

Mrs. Osgood sighed. "Okay, then, let's get this over with. Who's next?"

Bruce took his place at the end of the sidewalk and waved at the other boys. "Get in place," he told them. Without much enthusiasm, Mike, Tommy, and Lowell got down on their hands and knees in a line on the sidewalk, their heads tucked down. Bruce started skating far down the sidewalk so he could get up speed, and when he got to the three crouching boys, he leaped high to jump over them. He almost made it, coming down just a bit too soon and landing on Lowell's fingers. He didn't fall, though, and he finished with a fancy turn.

"Ow, God! You hit my hand!" Lowell said, standing up and shaking his fingers as if to throw off the pain.

"You're such a crybaby," Bruce said. "That was the most amazing jump ever!"

"And now we have two injured skaters," Mrs. Osgood said. "I really think—"

"We aren't stopping now!" Patsy said. "I'm the last one! Everybody out of my way!"

Patsy also gave herself a long start as she wheeled toward the side street. She was going incredibly fast, and Juliet knew she'd never be able to stop if a car came. And, Juliet suddenly realized, one *was* coming. She and Annette both screamed just as Patsy leaped off the curb, brought both legs up to the sides to touch her outstretched fingers, then landed and skated off not twenty yards in front of the approaching vehicle. The driver slammed on the brakes and stuck his head out the window.

"What's the matter with you? You wanna give me a heart attack?" he yelled.

Patsy grinned a little sheepishly. When the car passed, she skated back across the street to where her mother stood, openmouthed and quivering.

"Patricia Marie!" her mother said finally. "You could have been killed! Did you see that car?"

"I saw it, I saw it. I know what I'm doing. So, who won?"

"Won? Is that all you can think about? Let's get Juliet inside. I had no idea what you all were doing was so dangerous."

"But, Mom," Patsy insisted. "We have to know who won!"

"For goodness' sakes. All right then, *you* won, but you better never do anything like that again! The boy who jumped over the other boys is second. Then you, you, and you," she said, pointing to Lowell, Tommy, and Linda.

"I won!" Patsy shouted, then stopped to count up the points.

Bruce counted faster. "You might have won, but we got more points! We beat you, nine to six!"

"You should go home and put something on those cuts," Mrs. Osgood said to Lowell, who was blowing on his smashed-up fingers. "I don't like this game you children are playing. I think it should stop right now before someone gets badly hurt." She helped Juliet to her feet.

"We can't stop now," Patsy said. "There are still four tests left. And the boys are ahead—I'm not letting them win."

"I don't care who wins," Mrs. Osgood said. "I'm telling you to stop these tests."

But Juliet knew that no mere parent could stop this now. Patsy and Bruce wouldn't allow it. They were at war, and you didn't stop fighting a war just because you lost a few soldiers.

chapter fourteen

David ran ahead while the girls straggled into
the store behind a limping Juliet. Mrs. Osgood explained
the accident to Mr. and Mrs. Klostermeyer.

"It was part of this challenge thing the kids are doing,"
she said. "I've told Patsy I don't want her doing it anymore."

Neither of the Klostermeyers had paid much attention when Caroline had told them about the challenge,
but Juliet could tell they were embarrassed to admit that
to Mrs. Osgood. "We'll speak to Juliet about it too," Ethel
assured Mrs. Osgood.

Fortunately, Miss Reddinger, who was a nurse, was in
the store when Juliet hopped in.

"Let me take a look at it," she offered, following them
through the screen door and into the living room. Juliet lay
on the couch with the three women bending over her and
the three girls waiting impatiently in back of them. David
wandered around the room, running his hands over every
piece of furniture.

"Did she break it?" Linda asked.

"I don't think she's hurt too bad," Patsy said.

"How do you know?" Annette asked her.

"No breaks, Juliet, just a sprain," Miss Reddinger said. "Have you got an ice bag, Ethel? She should keep ice on it this evening, then wrap it in an Ace bandage overnight. You can give her an aspirin or two if it hurts. Stay off of it for twenty-four hours and it should be good as new."

"I told you," Patsy mumbled.

Ethel thanked everyone for their help, and the adults scooted the children outside, but not before Patsy whispered to Juliet. "You better be okay by tomorrow because we have to win the next one!"

Ethel rustled up an ice bag and some aspirin and then sat down next to her daughter. "What is this challenge Mrs. Osgood was talking about, and why don't I know about it?"

"It's no big deal," Juliet said. "It's just a test to see who's better, boys or girls." *And you don't know about it,* she thought, *because you're too busy to pay any attention to me.* But even as she thought it, she knew that in the past she'd more or less appreciated the fact that her mother was too preoccupied by her work to notice every little thing she did. Still, it would be nice if her mother was available when she *did* need somebody to talk to.

"What do you mean, who's better?" Ethel asked.

"You know, like who can hit a baseball the farthest,

who can run the fastest, who does the best tricks on skates. That kind of stuff." She left out the dog stunt; her mother wasn't likely to approve of that one. "It's not dangerous. I only fell down today because Patsy's little brother ran into me when I was standing on one leg."

"Well, it may not be dangerous, but it's pretty silly. Boys and girls can both be athletes. And they can both be clumsy klutzes, too."

"I know. It's just for fun," Juliet said, although she hadn't been enjoying it much herself.

"Maybe Mrs. Osgood is worried that Patsy will try some foolish stunt—she's such a tomboy," Ethel said. "If the kids dared each other to do something that wasn't safe, you'd come tell me, wouldn't you?"

Would she? Juliet nodded, well aware that she was making no verbal agreement. A mere shake of the head couldn't be construed as an actual promise. "Can I stay home from school tomorrow?"

"I guess you'll have to," Ethel said, sighing. "But I can't wait on you all day long. I have washing and ironing to do between customers." Juliet wondered if there was an ailment bad enough to keep her mother by her side for more than five minutes at a time. Would a broken leg do it? Or would it have to be polio?

✦

Juliet spent most of Thursday lying on the couch with her foot propped up on a pillow. Her ankle was much better when she got out of bed that morning, but she didn't admit it. It was nice to have one day when she didn't have to crawl underneath her desk or eat her sandwich with a lump in her throat.

She had the television on for a while, but the game shows kept being interrupted with special bulletins announcing that "U.S. military forces are prepared for war" and "the president has placed the blame for this crisis on the Soviet Union and its leaders." The announcers all wrinkled their foreheads and grimaced as they spoke. Then, as soon as the special report was over, commercials would come on with people singing "Let's have another cup of coffee" or telling you to "say good-bye to dry, flyaway hair." Juliet didn't see how anybody who'd just listened to the newscaster could give a darn about coffee or dry hair.

When her mother set up a TV tray with a bowl of tomato soup and a grilled cheese sandwich for lunch, Juliet asked her to turn the television off. She'd rather take a nap than listen to more special bulletins.

Ethel paused on her way out the door. "You aren't letting all this talk about bombs and war scare you, are you?"

Juliet shook her head as unconvincingly as possible. She knew what her answer was supposed to be, but surely her mother suspected the truth, that she was terrified.

"Good," Ethel said, a frown giving the lie to her words. "Worrying about it doesn't make the situation any better anyway."

Maybe not, Juliet thought, as she watched her mother hurry back to the store. *But I still wish you could sit here with me for a few minutes while we both pretend we're not worried.*

Patsy came by after school to bring Juliet her homework. "Is your ankle better?" she wanted to know. "We're supposed to meet at Bruce's house at three o'clock."

"I can walk on it okay, but I can't do tricks or anything. I could hit a baseball, but I can't run."

"Well, come anyway. We'll see what the test is—maybe you can do it."

"I thought your mom told you not to do any more tests."

"She told me not to, but I didn't say I wouldn't. She's busy with David—she'll never know. Besides, my dad thinks it's a good idea."

"You told your dad about it?"

"Yeah. He says competition is good."

"Does he think the girls can win?"

Patsy hesitated. "I don't think so. But that's okay, because he'll be all the more surprised when we do!"

Juliet walked gingerly through the store. "My ankle's better," she told her mother. "I'm going down to Patsy's." Since Patsy's mother didn't know the challenges were continuing, Juliet thought it better not to give her mother too much information either.

"Hold on!" Ethel said. "You're supposed to stay off your feet."

"Just for twenty-four hours, Miss Reddinger said. I'm okay now."

Ethel looked up doubtfully from the delivery of mops and cleaning products she was unpacking. "Well, be careful," she said. "Don't run!"

Patsy scuffed up rock dust as they walked down the alley. "I shouldn't have told the boys what yesterday's test was beforehand. Bruce practiced that darn jump—and now they're ahead of us."

"You were just trying to be fair."

"Well, I won't make that mistake again. Bruce was right about one thing—this is war. In war you don't have to be fair to your enemy."

"Our enemy? They aren't our *enemy*; they're just—"

"Which reminds me," Patsy continued, "we can't trust Annette anymore. She could be a spy for the boys."

"Couldn't Mike be a spy for the girls?" Juliet asked.

"I don't trust Mike, either."

"Patsy," Juliet began, remembering what her mother had said, "don't you think this is getting sort of . . . silly? Some people are good at one thing and some people are good at another. I mean, what does this challenge, or *war*, really prove?"

Patsy stopped walking and glared at Juliet. "How can you say that? We're proving that we're just as good as they are. Better, in fact! This is important! You can't give up!"

"I guess I forgot why it's so important."

Patsy blew up her cheeks with air and seemed about to explode. "Didn't you say that Lowell thought you weren't good enough to hang around with him and his friends? Well, we're proving we're good enough!"

"How is having a war with them going to make them want to hang around with us? Won't it just make them hate us more?"

"Who cares? At least they'll know we're better than them."

Is that what they'd think? Juliet doubted it. The boys would probably just say the girls had cheated or picked bad tests or something. They'd believe what they wanted to believe. But it was too hard to argue with Patsy. If there was one skill Patsy had mastered, it was winning an argument.

When they got to Bruce's backyard, both Mike and Tommy were talking to Annette, and Linda was standing with Lowell, looking a little self-conscious. Juliet shook her head. Linda was definitely barking up the wrong tree if she thought Lowell was interested in being somebody's boyfriend. They all looked up when Bruce emerged from his cellar door dragging an old, yellowed mattress.

"Could one of you jerks give me a hand with this?" he barked.

Tommy helped him pull the thing the rest of the way outside.

"What's that for?" Patsy asked.

"The test, which is climbing and jumping. It'll show who's a big, fat fraidy-cat and who isn't," Bruce said. "See that tree in the neighbors' yard? Whoever climbs the highest and then jumps down onto this mattress is the winner."

Bruce pointed to the tree behind Juliet's grandparents' house, the one she'd climbed a million times. The tree in which her grandfather had hung his bird feeders and wren houses. That tree was practically one of her relatives.

"Did you ask the people who live there if we could climb it?" Annette asked.

"They're both gone all day—they'll never even know."

"Who's the judge?" Mike asked.

"We don't need a judge," Bruce said. "Half you sissies probably won't even want to do it."

"What if you can climb high, but can't do the jump?" Linda wanted to know.

"Disqualified," Bruce said. "You have to jump. So, who's doing it? Besides me, of course."

"I can't," Juliet said. "I'd hurt my ankle again." It was too bad, too, because Juliet could climb that tree to the very top, and maybe she would have been able to do the jump, too. But she remembered Patsy bragging about her tree-climbing abilities, so at least they'd have one girl who could compete.

"Oh, Klostermeyer got hurt yesterday. Boo-hoo," Bruce said, rubbing his fists in his eyes.

"You should be glad she did," Lowell said. "She climbs like a monkey."

Before Bruce could comment on Lowell sticking up for the other side, Linda said, "I'll do it. I'm a good climber."

"I'm not," Annette said, looking at Mike. "Somebody could get hurt jumping from high up."

Patsy was staring into the top of the tree and pulling on a chunk of her unruly hair. "I'll . . . I'll do it," she said, without her usual excitement.

"So," Bruce said. "Two girls. How many boys?"

"Annette's right. This isn't safe," Mike said. "What if a limb breaks?"

Bruce rolled his eyes. "God, why don't you just go over to the girls' side with your little friend, Mikey? What a baby!"

"I'm not a baby. That mattress isn't very thick—"

"Are you doing it or not? Not that it matters—I'm going to win anyway."

Mike glanced at Annette. "No, I guess not." He looked at Tommy.

Tommy shrugged. "I guess I won't either, then."

"Lowell?" Bruce had a twisted smile on his face. "As if I had to ask."

"I'll . . . I'll give it a try," Lowell said.

Bruce looked surprised. "Whaddaya know, the princess has some guts after all!" They positioned the mattress so it was beneath the part of the tree with the thickest branches. Juliet had a feeling that that mattress would look awfully small from the top of the tree, but she was still sorry not to be able to show off something she was really good at. Instead she sat cross-legged on the grass and looked around the yard that didn't belong to her anymore.

Linda volunteered to go first. "I'm a pretty good climber," she said as she shinnied up the trunk and swung her leg over the first large branch. She got about halfway up the tree before she stopped to look down.

"Wow," she said. "I could climb higher, but I don't think I could jump down from farther up."

"Don't jump if you're afraid," Annette said. "It's not worth it."

"Don't listen to her!" Patsy yelled. "You can do it!"

"I know how to roll when I hit the ground," Linda assured them, and then she let go of the branch and leaped. She hit the mattress with her knees bent and rolled off to the side, then stood up triumphantly. "I did it!"

The girls were all impressed with Linda's jump, and Juliet could tell she was proud of being able to do a hard stunt.

Lowell started up the tree next.

"Come on, babyface," Bruce said. "All you have to do is jump from a low branch and you'll get points—there's only four of us."

Lowell wasn't a bad climber, but the jumping part would be difficult for him. Juliet wasn't surprised when he stopped climbing on the second branch up and jumped down. His landing wasn't as good as Linda's, and he limped a little afterward, but at least he'd done it.

Tommy looked fidgety. "Heck, I could jump from that low," he said. "That's no big deal."

"Do it then," Bruce said. "At least we'll get the extra points."

Tommy scaled the tree with ease and sailed off from the low branch without a problem. "Mike could do it too," he said.

Annette fixed Mike in her headlights. "He *could*, but he's being sensible," she said.

Mike's face turned red, and he looked away from them all, even Annette. "I guess I'm gonna, uh, skip this test," he said, shrugging.

Bruce snorted. "Man, I can't believe you're letting a girl tell you what to do! That is sick!" He shook his head and looked around. "Okay, then, it's just me and fuzzhead left."

"You go next," Patsy said to Bruce. She was twisting the hem of her jacket into a knot.

"Pay attention!" Bruce said. "Maybe you'll learn something." He began to climb the tree with ease. His longer legs gave him an advantage over the others, but his fearlessness helped him more. He was well past the spot Linda had stopped when he finally halted and looked down.

"That's too high to jump from," Mike said. "You'll get hurt."

"Oh, let him," Patsy said, as she chewed off one fingernail after another.

"I don't get hurt," Bruce bragged. Juliet remembered Patsy saying the same thing to her the first day they met. How had the two of them gotten so fearless?

Bruce took a deep breath and jumped. Annette couldn't look. It was a long way down, and the kids watching him didn't breathe until he hit the mattress on his tailbone and rolled over, hollering.

"Ow! Mary and Joseph!" he yelled, holding his lower back. He clambered to his feet quickly to show that he was tough and could take it, but he was obviously in pain and kept walking in circles trying to get rid of it. "Nobody can beat that jump!" he said through clenched teeth. "Stop looking at me, Patsy-Bratsy, and take your turn!"

Patsy walked up to the tree and put her hands on it. She peered up through the branches and shook her head as though to clear it. After a minute she shinnied up to the first branch and threw her leg over it. She sat there gripping the branch with her hands and knees both and looked down.

"What, are you having a spaz attack? Get going!" Bruce yelled.

Patsy closed her eyes for a minute, and when she opened them again, Juliet was shocked to see fear flashing in them, the emotion she'd been sure Patsy never felt. "I . . . I can't," Patsy finally said. "I'm afraid of heights. I'm dizzy! I have to get down!"

Juliet could hardly believe it—Patsy was afraid of something, and she was admitting it. She knew Patsy would be mad as a wet hen that she'd shown fear in front of everybody, but Juliet actually liked Patsy *more* now that she knew Patsy wasn't as brave as she pretended to be.

Bruce, of course, was delighted with this turn of events. He whooped and laughed while Juliet and Linda helped Patsy get back on solid ground. Her embarrassment turned into anger immediately. "I can't help it!" she said. "At least I tried, which is more than some people did!"

"But you didn't jump, Nervous Nelly, so you don't get any points," Bruce said happily. "I came in first, obviously, and then her and then Lowell and Tommy."

Linda tried not to look too happy about her performance, since the girls' team had lost, but Juliet could tell she felt pretty good about doing something even Patsy couldn't do.

"So, we've won four tests and you've won two. It's our turn to pick the test again, and if we win one more, we've won the war!" Bruce crowed.

"The challenge," Juliet said.

"And tomorrow's is going to be really good, so be prepared. Meet at Lowell's at the usual time."

"I think tomorrow's test should be more fair," Mike said. "No dangerous stuff that some people can't do. A different boy should come up with the idea instead of Bruce."

"I don't think so," Bruce said. "Because I already have a great idea. And don't worry, Mikey, you and your girlfriend won't get hurt doing it either. It's perfectly safe."

"It better be," Tommy said, sticking up for his brother.

Bruce just laughed at them all and dragged his dirty mattress back to his own yard. Everyone else shuffled back down the alley to Juliet's and Lowell's yards. Tommy told a few jokes, and everybody laughed except Patsy. Juliet had known Patsy just long enough to know there was probably a molten stream of anger bubbling away inside her waiting to boil over.

"Don't feel bad about the height thing, Patsy," Lowell said as the boys were about to peel off into his yard. "My mom has that too. She has to close her eyes when we drive over a bridge or anything."

"You don't have to feel sorry for *me*," Patsy exploded. "That was just one lousy test I couldn't do! I'm better at most of this stuff than all the rest of you combined!" Her look took in the boys and the girls.

"For Pete's sake!" Annette said. "He was just trying to be nice to you. You are the most conceited person I've ever met! Can't you just admit there are some things you aren't good at?"

"Yeah," Mike said. "I don't know how you girls put up with her."

Patsy's red cheeks paled, but for a change she kept her mouth shut.

Juliet felt she had to help Patsy out—she knew no one else would. "How can you guys put up with Bruce is what I want to know," she said. "He's rotten to the core."

"That's for sure," Linda agreed.

The three boys gave each other quick glances. "He's okay," Mike said.

Annette was shocked. "How can you say that? He's awful!"

The boys picked lint out of their pockets and stared at their shoes. Juliet knew the boys didn't like Bruce, but they'd never admit it. Did they think they had to stick up for him because he was their leader? Or, was this some loyalty thing boys had with each other that girls didn't? It made her feel awful that Lowell didn't have one bad thing to say about Bruce Wagner and, apparently, not one good thing to say about her.

"I'm going home," Annette said, picking her bike up off the ground. "I'm getting tired of being yelled at by Bruce *and* Patsy."

"Me too," Linda said.

"You better come back tomorrow!" Patsy said, her anger muted now.

"Maybe I will and maybe I won't!" Annette said. Then, just as she was leaving, she turned to Mike and said, "If you want to come over later, you can."

He grinned back at her.

"Oh, puke!' Patsy said as she turned on her heel. "I'm sick of the whole bunch of you!"

chapter fifteen

Hopelessness crept under the covers with Juliet that night as she lay in bed listening to her parents argue for hours about their financial problems.

"This idiotic Cuban thing has everybody on edge," Don fumed. "People are worried. They aren't spending their money."

"You're always looking for an excuse," Ethel said. "Somebody to blame your troubles on. Russia, Cuba, Democrats, supermarkets—"

"You tell me!" Don hollered back. "Were we doing this bad before that Kroger store opened on the highway? Were we? You tell me!"

"Our sales have been good this week. Everybody's buying canned goods to stockpile in their basement."

"That won't last! It just means they won't buy anything next week!"

Juliet and Caroline huddled under their blankets, neither of them able to sleep until after eleven o'clock, when their parents finally bickered their way to bed, exhausted.

Before she finally dropped off, Juliet prayed. *Dear God, please make my parents stop arguing so much. It's like they're having a war too. This war business is spreading over everything like poison ivy, and I'm getting tired of all the itching. Couldn't you dump a load of calamine lotion over the whole planet so everybody calms down for a while? That was kind of a joke, but I think you know what I mean.*

Morning came much too soon. While Caroline brushed her hair one hundred times, Juliet pulled herself out of bed and searched for a clean pair of socks. "How come Mom and Dad argue about money so much?" she asked.

Caroline shrugged. "I think all grown-ups argue about money. At least Mimi's parents do, and they have more of it than we do."

"I don't like being poor."

Caroline lowered her voice. "I heard Mom say she might have to look for a job as a bookkeeper if the store keeps losing money."

"How can she do that? Who would help Dad? He can't run the store all by himself!"

"I don't know, Juliet. I'm just telling you what I heard. Anyway, there're worse things to worry about than the store."

"The missiles in Cuba, you mean?" Juliet buttoned on a plaid, pleated skirt that needed ironing. She turned the flattened pleats to the back, where they'd just be sat on anyway.

Caroline nodded. "If a war starts, there won't even *be* a store to worry about." She banged her hairbrush down on her dresser. "I can't believe the adults are letting this happen to us. How do people get to be leaders of countries if they're stupid enough to build bombs that could kill everybody? It's not fair that we have to suffer for it."

Juliet didn't get it either, but she was surprised to be included as a "we" with her sister, no matter the reason.

"I guess we don't have enough money for a bomb shelter, either," she said.

"Dad would never get one anyway. He says they're worthless. Mimi's parents might get one, though—they're talking about it."

"Would she let you go in it with them if there was a war?"

Caroline shook her head. "No. There's only room for her and her brothers and her parents. There's never room for anybody but your own family."

Then, just as Juliet was guiltily feeling glad that Caroline wouldn't be the only Klostermeyer to live through a bomb attack, her sister surprised her again.

"Besides," Caroline said quietly, "I wouldn't want to be alive if my whole family was gone." She looked up at Juliet with eyes that threatened more leakage.

Juliet sat down next to Caroline on the bed. "Me either," she said, wondering how life could have changed so drastically in such a short time that the two of them were having this conversation.

"You should let me fix your hair sometime," Caroline said, gently fingering the uneven edges that hung over her sister's ears. "Don't let Mom give you any more permanents, or cut your hair either."

"I don't have money to go to a beauty shop."

"I'll cut it," Caroline said. "We'll grow out your bangs, too."

Juliet tried not to think about money or bombs or war as she ate breakfast, but the buttered toast seemed to expand in her mouth the more she chewed it, and she had to stretch her neck out to swallow it down.

The favorite topic among her classmates that day was what their parents had to say about the crisis. Juliet wished somebody would talk about something else, but most kids were eager to relay their parents' opinions, even the kids whose parents weren't Air Force. Some said the planes at Lathrop were already loaded with missiles and ready to take off at a moment's notice. Others said JFK had the whole situation under control already, and they wouldn't have to bomb Cuba even though they could. Still others bragged that their family's bomb shelters were stocked with enough peanut butter and comic books to take them through Christmas, so they didn't care if the bombs did fall—they'd get out of school and have a great time hiding out. Juliet could tell which kids were as scared as she was; they were the quiet ones who chewed their lips and said nothing.

As the girls walked out the front door of the school, a formation of military aircraft growled through the sky overhead, and they all looked up. Was this just the usual exercises or were they going somewhere—like Cuba? Juliet didn't want to know.

"My dad says everything will turn out fine, and I believe him," Patsy said as they retrieved their bicycles and put up the kickstands.

"How come it's on the TV all day and night, then?" Annette said. "President Kennedy doesn't think it's fine."

"You said Mike isn't worried, though," Linda reminded her.

"I know, but all the Lathrop kids say that. They *have* to."

"No, we don't," Patsy said. "It's the truth! My dad says—"

"Just because your dad says it doesn't make it true," Annette said.

Juliet rolled her bike up next to Annette's. "Do you think we're going to have a chance to grow up?"

For a minute they all stared at her, but nobody said a word.

"What?" Patsy finally spat out.

"My sister Caroline says we might not grow up and get

married like our parents. Because the world will end before that."

Linda's face began to collapse. "What a horrible thing to say!"

"Geez!" Patsy said. "That's the dumbest thing I ever heard. The United States isn't going to let that happen!"

Annette shivered. "If I thought that was true, I'd die right now. It would be too sad to live."

"Not that I want to get married anyway," Patsy said. "Boys are idiots."

"No, they're not!" Linda and Annette were happy to leap away from the topic of death and destruction and onto the subject of boys. "You just think that because you aren't ready to date them yet," Annette said. "You'll change your mind someday."

"No, I won't."

"You just haven't matured yet," Linda said.

"I hope I never *do* if it means I have to marry a boy!"

Just because her friends didn't want to talk about it didn't mean Juliet could stop thinking about it. She could still hear the jets roaring in the distance, and she sent up a quick prayer: *Dear God, please don't let the world end today.* Surely that wasn't too much to ask. She just had to remember to ask it every day from now on.

When they got to her house, Juliet went inside to change into blue jeans. She took her time getting back outside; she wasn't looking forward to whatever plan Bruce had come up with. It couldn't be good. People had gotten injured both of the last two days, and even though Bruce was one of them, she knew he was bound to come up with a plan even more outrageous than the ones before.

Juliet wished they could just stop the challenge now, but she didn't know how to make that happen. She knew that neither Patsy nor Bruce would give in, and everybody else was afraid to look cowardly by admitting they wanted to quit. So the challenges would continue for three more days. Unless a bomb went off, in which case there wouldn't be any winners.

"Took you long enough," Bruce said when Juliet showed up. "We have to take a short walk before we can do the test."

"Where to?" Patsy asked.

"You'll see." Bruce smirked and gave a little laugh.

"How did you get to be so annoying?" Patsy said, as the girls fell in line behind the boys.

"Born lucky, I guess." He swaggered down the sidewalk at the head of the pack.

By the end of the first block Annette and Mike had fallen to the back. They were walking so close to each other that their sleeves brushed together, and from time to time a stray finger reached out and touched the other person's hand.

Patsy turned around and gave them a dirty look. "We should stick with our own team members."

"That's just your stupid rule," Annette said. "Nobody else cares."

A few blocks more and they were at the corner where Abbott Street met Route 47. Bruce turned into a parking lot right before the corner and stopped walking. Before them stood the recently opened Kroger supermarket, the very store that Juliet's father claimed was putting Klostermeyer's out of business.

"I can't go in there," Juliet said immediately.

"Why? Your ankle wasn't too sore to walk down here," Bruce said. "You don't even know what the test is yet."

"I can't go into a supermarket," she said. "I promised my dad."

"What kind of test can you do in a supermarket anyway?" Lowell asked.

A wicked smile lit up Bruce's face. He leaned forward and whispered, "Shoplifting."

"What the Sam Hill?" Linda shook her head. "There's no way I'm doing that. You can get arrested!"

"Me either," Annette said. "You're crazy."

"Oh, for Pete's sake," Patsy said. "It's not that big of a deal. I've done it before. Even if they catch you, they just throw you out—they don't arrest kids! What do we have to take?"

Everybody stared at Patsy. "You've *done* it?" Annette asked.

"Don't have a cow," Patsy said, waving away the other girl's concerns.

Juliet was stunned by Patsy's admission—not only had she stolen things before, but she didn't seem to think there was anything much wrong with it. Would Patsy steal from Klostermeyer's, too? Had she already? Juliet's father had caught a boy shoplifting last summer, and he'd thrown him out the front door onto the sidewalk. If he knew Juliet was standing there even *thinking* about stealing, he would paddle her good.

Bruce continued with his rules. "You have to take something that would help you survive in a war. Say the Commies landed at Lathrop and it was every man for himself."

"That won't happen," Mike said.

"Anyway," Tommy said, "you can't get guns in a supermarket."

"Not guns, you moron. Think about it for two seconds. What would you need to keep yourself alive? If you get caught, your whole team loses. Whoever takes the most useful thing is the winner."

Annette pulled on Mike's arm. "You're not doing this, are you?"

"God Almighty," Bruce said, turning on Mike. "Are you gonna let her keep telling you what to do?"

Mike looked uncomfortable. "It's not such a big deal," he said to Annette.

"You haven't done it before, have you?"

"No, but–" He shook off her hand. "I can do it."

"I'll do it too," Tommy said, loyal as ever.

Lowell nodded his head unhappily. "Okay."

"Lowell!" Juliet said. "You're going inside a super-market?"

"Geez, Juliet, we're not going to be struck dead for just stepping inside the place!"

The shoplifting was only a secondary concern for Juliet; it was walking through the front door that was fraught with terror for her. What if her father happened to be making a delivery to the Lombardis and his truck came down the street just as she was going inside? Or what if she ran into one of her parents' customers shopping at Kroger? That would be humiliating for all of them. And even if nobody saw her, *she'd* know she'd done the one thing her father had made her promise never to do. Still, there was a part of her that was very curious to see what lay beyond those big double doors. And Lowell was going to go inside and see!

"We quit!" Annette announced as she and Linda headed for the street. "This whole challenge is getting too dangerous–and Patsy and Bruce are nuts!"

Patsy kicked the nearest tire and turned on the two

girls. "You traitors! I shoulda known I couldn't trust you. Go ahead, make like a tree and leave!"

Annette took one final look at Mike, but he was suddenly busy studying the sale posters plastered in the store windows. Linda tugged on Annette's sleeve, and they disappeared up Abbott Street.

"Juliet, come on," Patsy said. "You can't let me down. All the boys are going to do it—I can't be the only girl!"

Bruce seemed barely to register Annette and Linda's departure. "We can't all go in together," he said. "That'll make 'em suspicious. You three guys go together, and then you two girls, and I'll go in last, by myself. I don't need any accomplices."

Mike and Tommy nodded, but they looked awfully self-conscious as they walked through the sliding doors, and Lowell, behind them, looked ready to pass out.

After a minute or two Bruce said, "Okay, you two go now."

Patsy grabbed Juliet's elbow.

"I can't!" Juliet said.

"You have to!" Patsy hissed. "Look at it this way—you're hurting Kroger if you shoplift from them. So that's a good thing, right? Your dad would be *proud* of you!"

Juliet knew that wasn't true, but she found herself following her friend anyway.

As Patsy propelled her toward the door, she whispered,

"Don't you want to show the boys you aren't a scaredy-cat? Just take something small to prove you can do it, then walk out. And don't act suspicious!"

Juliet continued to make protesting noises, but she didn't really fight Patsy. The closer she got to the door of the store, the more she wanted to go in. What would it be like in there? Could the entire store really be full of food? What did they have that Klostermeyer's Market didn't have? This was her chance to find out.

Juliet walked through the door into the devil's head-quarters.

chapter sixteen

Once she was inside Kroger, Juliet's mouth dropped open. There were *three* checkout counters at the front of the store, each with a woman behind a cash register ringing up purchases and a boy putting the food into brown bags. Customers pushed big baskets on wheels up and down the aisles. One of the bag boys rolled a basket to the door while a customer followed along behind. At Klostermeyer's if the customer had too many groceries to carry out to the car alone, Juliet's dad carried them out himself.

Patsy went straight to the candy counter, but Juliet was so amazed by her surroundings that she immediately forgot the reason she was there in the first place. She wandered down one of the many aisles, amazed by the variety of food. There must have been twenty kinds of cereal in Kroger, not just the Cheerios, Rice Krispies, and Corn Flakes her parents stocked. The cookie aisle was filled with brands she'd seen on television but never in person. There was milk from two different dairies, and bottled chocolate milk, which she hadn't known existed. There was even a choice of three different brands of toilet paper. Juliet couldn't imagine why you needed so many kinds of *that*.

She wandered back to the meat counter, behind which the men were all dressed in the same kind of long white apron her father always wore. She'd often heard her parents say it was the meat that kept their customers coming in. Supposedly, Klostermeyer's meat was fresher than you could get at a supermarket, and her father's skills as a butcher also made it somehow superior. But here they had *three* men, and all of them seemed to know what they were doing, and the meat looked just fine.

The despair Juliet had awoken with came crawling back into her heart. How could Klostermeyer's ever compete with stores like this? They had ten aisles! Freezers and refrigerator cases took up long walls and held products she'd never even heard of. What was yogurt? There was more food here than Juliet had ever seen in one place before—you could spend hours just looking at it. And people would, she knew. Even *she* wished she could shop here.

Patsy came hurrying up to Juliet as she stood gaping at a large display of potato chips. "What are you doing? We have to get out of here!"

Slowly, Juliet followed Patsy back to the front door, her eyes lingering on the overflowing bins of apples and oranges as she passed by. Once they were outside, Patsy spotted Lowell gesturing to them from the Abbott Street side of the building, and she sauntered casually in that direction. Juliet kept stopping and turning around to look back at Kroger, but finally they were both out of sight of the door.

"Sorry we took so long," Patsy said. "Juliet got hypnotized in there."

"Bruce isn't out yet," Mike said. "I think he wants to take cigarettes, but they're right up at the front counter."

"What'd you take?" Patsy asked.

The twins both stuck their hands in their jacket pockets and pulled out small spiral notebooks and pencils that said KROGER FOOD STORES.

"Pencils?" Patsy said. "What for?"

"Pencils and paper," Tommy said. "To write notes to people. The phones might not work."

Patsy rolled her eyes. "What did you get, Lowell?"

Lowell was chewing on his thumbnail and didn't look up. "Nothing," he said.

"Nothing? You didn't take anything?"

"I couldn't," he said. "It didn't feel right."

"Or maybe you just chickened out," Patsy said.

"I didn't take anything either," Juliet said. "I forgot."

"Yes, you did!" Patsy said, laughing. "Look in your pocket!"

Juliet reached hesitantly into her jacket pocket, as though

there might be a mousetrap inside waiting to be sprung. Instead, she pulled out a Zero bar.

"You put a candy bar in my pocket?"

"Sure. I got one for me too. I remembered you liked Zero bars."

"I do, but . . ." Her legs felt suddenly weak—what if she'd been caught shoplifting at Kroger? Her father would never have forgiven her. How could she even have gone into that store after all the times her father had told her not to? The candy bar in her hand felt as heavy as a butcher knife and twice as sharp.

"You took candy bars?" Mike said. "How is that better than paper and pencils?"

"You can eat them, dumbo. Besides, I also took these." She lifted up her jacket and pulled a pair of scissors from the waistband of her jeans and dangled them in front of the group. "You could stab somebody with these!"

A sudden ruckus in front of the store interrupted their show-and-tell.

"I've had enough of your shenanigans!" a man yelled. "You're cruisin' for a bruisin', boy! I'm calling the police if I ever catch you in here again! And don't think I'm not gonna call your mother! I don't know how that poor woman got stuck with a kid like you!"

A heavyset man in a white shirt had hold of Bruce by both arms and was shaking him like a rag doll. Bruce didn't look so brave with the angry man towering above him, screaming and spitting in his face. When the man let go of one arm, Bruce held it up over his face as though he expected to be struck.

"I ain't gonna hit ya," the man said. "I ain't your old man. I'm beginning to see why he took off, though. If I had to come home to a brat like you every day, I'd get mighty sick of it too!"

Patsy peeked around the corner of the building. "Mary and Joseph! Bruce got caught! Let's get out of here so they don't see us with him!" She took off up Abbott Street, and the others pounded along behind her.

A few blocks later, as they approached Lowell's yard, they slowed down, breathing heavily.

"We won!" Patsy crowed as she jumped around in circles. "Bruce got caught and the girls won!"

Bruce was only a little way behind the rest of them. When they turned to watch him approach, he tried to rearrange his features into a smirking grin, but he was not entirely successful. Juliet thought she saw a quiver in his usually stony, stubborn jaw.

"Man, did you see that guy?" Bruce said with an exaggerated laugh. "He was so mad he was practically wetting his pants."

"You think getting thrown out of a store is funny?" Lowell asked.

Bruce sneered at Lowell but didn't answer his question.

"What were you trying to take?" Mike asked.

"Cigarettes. I really wanted them too. The manager is onto me at that place—I have to find a new store."

"What do cigarettes have to do with surviving a war?" Patsy asked.

"The cigarettes were what got me caught," Bruce said. "These are what I took for survival." He pulled a box of matches from his jacket pocket. "You can start a fire with them if you're cold, or you can burn down your enemy's house. Lots of uses."

"Anyway, you got caught, so girls win," Patsy said. "I stole scissors."

"Not bad," Bruce conceded, his confidence returning, "but there's two more tests and only two girls left. I wouldn't count my chickens if I were you. And don't pick some sissy thing for tomorrow either. Pick a test that's really a test. Something that proves who's brave and who's not."

"We have to go to our grandmother's in the morning," Mike said. "Can the test be in the afternoon?"

"Yeah, I'm going to the base with my dad in the morning. So let's meet here at one o'clock," Patsy said.

As they walked back to her house, Juliet heard Bruce say to the boys, "So, tomorrow, after the test, how about we go to the go-kart track?"

If it had been anybody but Bruce, Juliet might have

felt bad for him having to beg to be included. There was some mumbling from the other boys, but nobody said, "Sure, you can come with us." Of course they didn't want him to go along with them. But Juliet knew they'd probably let him go anyway, because it was too hard to say no to Bruce. They'd had no problem telling *her* to get lost, but they wouldn't argue with a bully they didn't even like. How brave was *that*?

Patsy polished off her candy bar as they sat on the front steps of Klostermeyer's Market.

"Aren't you going to eat yours?" she asked Juliet.

"Not right now. My stomach feels funny."

"I feel great," Patsy said. "The two of us alone beat all the boys!"

"Only because Bruce got caught," Juliet said. "Otherwise his matches might have beaten your scissors."

"They would not, either!" Patsy threw the candy bar wrapper on the sidewalk. "You know, sometimes you really bug me, Juliet. We won. You should be happy!"

Juliet couldn't remember the last time she'd felt happy. Before Lowell had stopped being her friend, before the Russians had missiles aimed at them, before the war between the boys and the girls. It seemed like ages ago.

"I hate to say it," Patsy said, "but I think Bruce is right. We have to do something to prove to the boys that we're as brave as they are. Now that we've gotten rid of Annette and Linda, we can do something harder . . . something *scary*."

"We didn't exactly 'get rid' of Annette and Linda, you know. They quit."

"So? Who needs them? If we come in first and second, we'll win anyway."

Coming in first and second would mean both of them beating Bruce, which was pretty unlikely. But Juliet knew that if she said that, Patsy would get angry again.

"The shoplifting was a good idea," Patsy said. "It got rid of the sissies. Bruce didn't even care that he lost, because getting thrown out of the store kind of made him the hero anyway. We have to think of something else like that."

Juliet wasn't sure Patsy was right about Bruce not caring, but she didn't argue the point. "I don't want to steal anything," she said. "And no more supermarkets, either!"

"Okay, okay, no stealing, no supermarkets. How about . . . is there a haunted house around here anywhere? You know, someplace nobody lives that's old and scary."

Juliet swallowed hard. She didn't like to be scared. "Not a house, but there's an old barn a few blocks away. The farmer died, and his family doesn't farm anymore, and the place is falling down. It's not near the house, either—it's down the road."

"But is it really scary?"

"If you go inside and close the doors, it's completely dark. There are skunks in there sometimes and lots of spiders. I've seen bats, too. There's a hayloft with a rickety old ladder up to it. Last year some high school kids used it for a haunted house at Halloween, and they left some stuff in there too—like a skeleton with one leg hanging from a beam."

Patsy nodded. "That sounds pretty good. Let me think about it."

Thank goodness there were only two tests left, and then they could stop all this boys against the girls stuff, Juliet thought. She didn't even care who won anymore. And though she hated to admit it, she was beginning to think that Patsy was a little too bossy for a best friend. She missed Lowell more than ever.

Ethel had gone to the nursing home to visit her mother that afternoon and had been too busy to cook a decent meal, so the family took their frozen TV dinners into the living room. The last few nights they'd eaten on TV trays while watching the evening news, yet another hindrance to Juliet's digestion. She dipped her chicken leg into the mashed potato section of the tin to coat it with gravy, then licked the gravy off without actually eating any meat. She intended to bypass the mixed vegetables entirely, if she could get away with it, and just eat the mashed potatoes and the chocolate pudding.

As usual the news started with the latest on what the newsman called "the Cuban missile crisis." But the report didn't seem quite as dire as it had the past few nights.

"Soviet Premier Nikita Khrushchev today sent a message to President Kennedy in which he promised to remove missiles from Cuba if President Kennedy will publicly announce that the U.S. will never invade Cuba."

"That's good!" Caroline said, turning to her parents. "Isn't it? Does that mean it's over?"

"It could be good news," Ethel said. "I think it's too early to know for sure."

"You can't trust that Khrushchev any farther than you can throw him," their father said. "Besides, Kennedy can't make a promise like that."

"I don't see why he can't," Ethel said. "If it brings this to an end."

Don shook his head. "You don't know anything about politics."

"I know as much as you do!" Ethel shot back.

Don looked disgustedly at the chicken leg he'd just bitten into and then dropped it into the dessert section of his dinner tray. "God Almighty, this chicken is cold! I don't know why people want to eat this frozen crap!"

Ethel sighed and got up. "I'm sorry I'm not Wonder Woman. I'll make you a sandwich," she said, removing the tray from in front of her husband.

"Salami and Swiss on rye," he said. "And bring me a cup of coffee while you're out there."

"Yes, Your Majesty," Ethel said as she trudged from the room.

Suddenly, Juliet's chicken didn't taste so bad. Maybe because the war might not be starting after all. Or maybe because her father was being such a pill about eating *his* food, and she didn't want her mother to feel bad for making frozen dinners. Whatever the reason, she demolished her drumstick in no time flat and ate two bites of vegetables before scraping every last ounce of chocolate pudding from the tin.

Caroline's appetite seemed to have improved too. When they were finished, the older girl took her younger sister's tray to the kitchen with her own and even smiled as she did it.

chapter seventeen

Juliet slept late Saturday morning and woke up feeling better than she had in days. Over breakfast Caroline asked her if she'd mind if Mimi came over in the afternoon to play records. She *asked* her.

"Don't worry," Juliet said. "I have plans with Patsy this afternoon."

Caroline looked up from her cereal. "You're not still doing that challenge thing, are you?"

It didn't feel right to lie to Caroline just when her sister was being nicer to her. "We only have two more to do, and then it's over," she said. "Unless the boys win today; then they win the whole thing."

"Why does it matter who wins?"

"We have to prove we're just as good as they are."

"But I don't see how races and skating contests prove anything."

Juliet sighed. She wasn't sure anymore either. "It matters a lot to Patsy."

"Well, don't let Patsy or Bruce talk you into doing something dangerous."

"I won't," she said, hoping it was true.

Around eleven Annette called. "I was just wondering what happened yesterday."

"Didn't Mike tell you?"

Annette hesitated. "He didn't call me, and I was afraid to call him. Do you think he's mad at me?"

"I don't know," Juliet said. "He had to go to his grandmother's this morning—maybe he was just too busy to call."

"Maybe." Annette sighed. "So, did you and Patsy steal anything?"

"She stole a scissors and two candy bars, but I didn't take anything. It was so strange to be inside that huge store."

"So, I guess the boys won."

"Nope. Bruce got caught and was kicked out, so we won."

"Oh, my gosh! Really? It serves him right. Mike didn't get caught, did he?"

"No. Mike and Tommy only took pencils and notebooks. Probably nobody even cares if you take a few pencils. Lowell didn't take anything either."

"I'm glad nobody got caught but Bruce."

"What about Patsy? Do you wish she'd gotten caught?"

There was no sound on the other end of the line for a minute. "Not really," Annette said finally. "I know she's your friend, Juliet, and sometimes I can even see why you like her. She can be kind of kooky and fun, but sometimes she really bugs me. She's the kind of person my dad calls a 'loose cannon.' You never know what she's going to do or say. She's a little bit crazy, and a little bit of a liar, too. At least I think so."

Juliet had to agree. A little bit of a liar was exactly what Patsy was.

"Anyway, Linda has to clean her room today, and I don't have anything to do. Do you think I could come over this afternoon?"

"You mean be on the team again?"

"No, I don't want to do any more tests, especially since Bruce and Patsy cook them all up. Each one is worse than the one before. I just thought I'd come to cheer you on or something."

"Cheer *us* on or cheer Mike on?"

"I don't know. Maybe both. I miss him, Juliet. He was my first boyfriend."

It sounded like Annette might be working herself up for a good cry, and Juliet was not interested in listening to that. "You can come if you want to," she said. "We're meeting here at one o'clock."

Annette sniffed. "Thanks. You don't think Patsy will mind?"

"Oh, she probably will, but she doesn't run the world."

Annette laughed. "Even if she thinks she does."

Juliet felt disloyal for snickering about Patsy with

Annette. In two weeks she'd gone from thinking Patsy was her best friend to talking about her behind her back. From now on, she promised herself, she would speak up when she disagreed with Patsy. If they were going to continue to be friends, Juliet would have to start telling her how she really felt.

She was just about to go downstairs and wait for Patsy when Caroline and Mimi burst into the bedroom, their usual excited chatter heightened by a kind of frantic emotion.

Caroline grabbed Juliet's arm. "We just heard it on the radio! Now there's going to be a war for sure!"

"I don't know why your father won't build you a bomb shelter!" Mimi shrieked. "You have to have one!"

"What happened?" Juliet asked, fear already squeezing her insides like two fists on a washrag.

Caroline's eyes jumped with panic. "An American plane was shot down over Cuba!"

"A U-2," Mimi put in. "A spy plane!"

"The Russians will be mad that we were spying on them, and the U.S. will be mad because they shot down our plane!"

"What happened to the pilot? Was he from Lathrop?" Juliet asked.

"They didn't say." Mimi's eyes were round as baseballs.

"I can't believe this," Caroline howled. "I thought every-thing was getting better!"

"You have *got* to get a bomb shelter!" Mimi persisted. "Can't you talk to your dad?"

"We can't afford one," Juliet said. "Besides, what if you aren't even home when the bomb hits? What if you're over here and you can't get home in time?"

The sudden anxiety on Mimi's usually smug face made Juliet feel better for a few seconds. But not for long. She saw now how foolish her own relief of the day before had been. She'd let down her guard too soon. She'd trusted the news reporters to know what they were talking about, but did they? Did anybody really know what was going on? Maybe if you were sitting next to JFK in the Oval Office, or if you had lunch with Khrushchev at the Kremlin, you'd have some idea, but everybody else in the world had to go around feeling sick and scared all the time, constantly wondering if that roar in the sky was just another plane from Lathrop or a missile on its way from Cuba.

Juliet didn't know how much longer she could stand worrying like this. How could she go to school and do multiplication tables and read stories about dogs and birthday parties as if nothing was ever going to change? It could change in an hour. It could all be over in a minute. She opened the drawer of her bedside table and took out the pieces of the cup that had belonged to her grandpa. If the whole world was suddenly broken to pieces, the cup would be the least of her sorrows. *God, how could you let this get so bad? I've been talking to you about it all week, and you haven't done anything to help. I have decided you could not possibly be real.*

Juliet felt bereft even thinking such a thing. If there was no God, the world would certainly not be saved. And without God who would she tell about all the worries that plagued her?

Suddenly, an image of the God she'd been praying to these past weeks and months rose in her mind, the God she was letting go of. To her immense surprise Juliet recognized him. It was her grandpa. Her imagination had draped him in a long white cloak, but there was no mistaking that shock of silver hair or the deep blue eyes she'd always trusted. If she'd really been praying all along to Grandpa, she knew he'd do what he could to help her. Unless, like God, he no longer existed.

Juliet dragged herself downstairs. As she walked through the store, she heard some customers talking about the downed airplane too. She hurried outside so she wouldn't have to listen to their nervous voices.

Patsy was already sitting on the front step. She didn't even look up. "I guess you heard?"

Juliet nodded.

"I was at the base with my dad. One of the officers told us." Unlike everybody else Patsy didn't sound scared, but she didn't sound like herself, either.

"Was the plane from Lathrop?"

"No. It was from Florida somewhere."

"That's good, I guess."

Finally Patsy looked up, her face blotchy. "The officer took Dad and me to see an underground bomb shelter. A big one, with all kinds of food and stuff. People could stay there for a long time."

Juliet thought if she heard one more thing about bomb shelters she would scream. She sighed. "So, that's where you'd go if we were being attacked?"

Patsy picked absentmindedly at the laces of her tennis shoes. Her voice came out stiff, thick. "No. There wouldn't be time. Only the people on base go there. Not their families. There isn't enough room. My dad would go there if he was at work when the bomb came. He'd be safe, but the rest of us would die!" Tears rolled down Patsy's face.

Juliet was unprepared for this: Tough, strong, fearless Patsy was crying.

"But didn't you say your dad wasn't worried? He said there wouldn't be any war!"

Patsy rubbed her face with the sleeve of her sweatshirt. "That's what he *said*, but I don't believe him anymore. Why would they have a bomb shelter at Lathrop if they didn't think they'd need it? Besides, I've been on air bases my whole life, and I've never seen people look as worried as they do now. Nobody is joking around or having fun or anything. They think there's going to be a war, and you know what that means."

Juliet did. "We don't have a bomb shelter either," she reminded Patsy.

Patsy snorted. "Great. We can all blow up together."

chapter eighteen

Juliet and Patsy sat on the step staring forlornly at the sidewalk that stretched out in front of them.

"Wait here," Juliet said. She got to her feet and went into the store. There were three customers, all yakking away, so her parents were busy and didn't see her stick her hand in the candy case and pull out two Zero bars.

Outside again, she handed one to Patsy. It was the only thing she could think of to cheer her up a little.

"Thanks," Patsy said, but didn't immediately rip off the wrapper as she usually did. "So, did you steal these?" she asked, pointing the bar at Juliet.

"Steal them? No. I just took them."

"What's the difference?"

"The difference is my parents own the store!"

Patsy looked up at Juliet with the shadow of a smile playing across her face. "Did they see you take them? Did you tell them you were taking candy bars?"

"No."

"Then it's stealing."

Annette was right, Juliet thought. Sometimes Patsy made you so mad you wanted to smack her. And just when she'd been feeling sorry for her too! Well, she didn't intend to let Patsy get away with being mean anymore. "Are you trying to start a fight with me?" she asked.

Patsy shrugged. "No. I'm just saying you're not so perfect all the time either."

"I never said I was!"

"You act like it, though. You're so nice all the time—you want everybody to like you."

"What's wrong with that?" Juliet was truly stumped.

"It makes other people feel bad!" Patsy yelled. She got up from the step and took a deep breath. "I know you're nicer than I am, but that doesn't mean you're so darn perfect! You took the candy bars without asking, and that's stealing!"

Juliet knew Patsy was a little bit right, but it made her furious anyway, and she leaped to her feet too. "Well, at least I don't *lie* like you do!" she said. "You told me the first day I met you that you were some kind of great tree climber, but then it turns out you can't climb a tree at all. And you said you were allergic to dog bites, when you're really just scared of dogs! You've probably told me other lies too, and I just don't know about them yet."

Patsy looked her square in the face. "I probably have," she said. "I lie a lot."

In the face of this admission Juliet's anger evaporated. "Why? I don't care if you can climb trees or not. And everybody was afraid of Boneguard."

"You said you were such a good tree climber. I wanted you to think I was as good as you were. I hate being scared of things. I don't want anybody to think I'm a sissy."

"Nobody would think that. Besides, you're better than me at most things—you're a faster runner, and you can hit a ball farther, skate better. What difference does it make if I'm better at one or two things?"

Patsy turned and walked toward the alley. "I don't know, but I just have to be better at everything. I have to."

"No, you don't."

"Yes, I do," Patsy said. "Especially at all that boy stuff. Come on. They're all over at Lowell's house already."

Juliet was stunned. She realized that much of what Patsy bragged about might well be lies—being bitten by dogs, punching a boy in the face—but what she'd just told her was definitely the truth. Patsy *had* to win.

Just as the two groups met in the alley, Annette rode up on her bike. She gave a little wave and sneaked a peek at Mike. He waved back at her but said nothing.

"What are you doing here?" Patsy asked her. "I thought you quit."

"I did. I just came over to watch."

Patsy shrugged and said nothing, surprising everyone.

She started down the alley, listlessly kicking rocks. "We have to walk a few blocks to where the test is. I'll tell you about it when we get there."

Bruce was full of his usual bravado about winning, but the rest of the group was subdued as they followed Patsy. Tommy told a few jokes, but nobody laughed much. Juliet wondered if things like jokes or cartoons would ever seem funny again. If anything would. Even Boneguard was quiet as they passed, giving a few measly woofs and retreating to the porch step.

Lowell walked beside Juliet. "My mom is really upset," he said. "She went back to bed when she heard about the plane being shot down."

Juliet nodded. "It's Caroline who's going crazy at our house," she told him. "She's like a faucet you can't turn off."

Mike heard them talking. "Oh, man, you should have seen our grandma this morning. Dad transferred to Lathrop to be closer to her, but now Grandma wants to move in with us, she's so scared."

"And there's no room for her in our house!" Tommy said.

Mike nodded. "Dad told her they aren't going to bomb us and she should stop worrying, but I guess she can't."

"Do you think your dad's right?" Juliet asked him.

Mike glanced at his brother. "I don't know. We were talking about it this morning. I hope he is."

"Well, if a bomb hits, your dad'll be safe on the air base, but you won't. Tell Grandma *that*!" Patsy said.

Behind her back Mike made the swirly finger sign by his ear that meant he thought Patsy was crazy.

"Do you think it's going to happen, Juliet?" Lowell asked.

"I do," she said. "I wish I didn't, though."

"Yeah, me too."

"Are we going to that old barn?" Annette asked as they approached the big, sagging building overgrown with weeds. "Ooh, I hate that place. I'm glad I'm not doing this test!"

"Yeah, we're glad too," Patsy said as the group tromped through the weeds to reach the barn door.

"I went to a haunted house in there once. It's really creepy!" Annette continued. "There are real bats in there!"

"That's what I hear," Patsy said. "And maybe skunks and raccoons and rats and spiders and God knows what all. The test is we go inside and close the door so it's as dark as possible. And we stay there. The last person out is the winner, and that team wins."

Bruce gave a mocking laugh. "Are you kidding? I could sit in that place all day. I'm not afraid of skunks and spiders!"

"Neither am I!" Patsy said.

Nobody else claimed to be fearless, but they all followed Patsy inside. Just before the door closed them into the dark, Juliet saw Annette lift the handle on an old well hand pump and stick her mouth underneath for a drink. She wished she could stay outside with Annette, but then again what difference did it make? If she really believed a bomb was going to explode any day now and destroy her whole life, why should she be afraid of a skunk or a bat? Why be afraid of anything besides that one last moment?

The skeleton Juliet remembered from her last visit to the barn was now missing all its leg bones, which didn't make it any less creepy. At least she hadn't seen any bats on the ceiling. The two teams sat down on the packed dirt floor. It wasn't completely dark inside; light leaked through a few spaces where the boards on the sides of the building had broken or worn away. It wasn't enough light to make you feel comfortable in there, though.

At first nobody said anything. Juliet closed her eyes and breathed in the smell of hay and cows that still lingered in the barn; she'd always found those warm smells comforting. Just when she'd started to relax a little, she heard a squeaking noise, but it only took a few seconds to realize it must be coming from Bruce rather than from an animal.

"Shut up, Bruce," Patsy said.

"You didn't say we had to be quiet," he reminded her.

"Shut up anyway," Mike said.

"Who are you telling to shut up?" Bruce was always ready to get angry at the drop of a hat.

"You!" Patsy said. "I want to be able to hear it when the rats start to chew your face off."

Juliet wished she didn't have *that* image stuck in her brain now. But after a few minutes of sitting in the dark her eyes began to adjust to it, and she could see Patsy and Lowell, who were sitting nearest to her, quite well. The longer they sat there, the more she could see. Which probably meant that any animals in the barn could see them too and weren't likely to come sniffing around. She had to admit it wasn't all that frightening in there. How long were they going to have to sit in the dirt until people got up and left?

Apparently, Bruce was thinking the same thing.

"This is stupid!" he said. "It's not even scary. You can't even come up with a good test!"

Patsy turned and glared at Juliet. "It wasn't my idea," she said. "I thought it would be darker."

Bruce jumped up. "Where are the skunks and rats and stuff?" He poked through a few stalls, kicking the walls and calling, "Come on out, rats!" Then he found the old ladder to the hayloft and shook it. "What's up here?"

"Hay," Juliet said. "What else?"

"Let's go up!" he said, not waiting for anybody to join him.

"I hope the ladder breaks," Patsy said.

Bruce was up and into the loft in seconds. "There's still a bunch of hay up here!" he said.

"That makes it a lot scarier," Mike said.

Suddenly Bruce barked out a laugh that gave Juliet the creeps. "I've got an idea. I'm gonna make this test into a *real* war!"

They all looked up at Bruce as he pulled the box of matches from his pocket.

"This barn has just been firebombed by Russian planes!" he yelled as he lit a match and threw it into the nearest hay bale. "*Now* the last person out is the winner!"

chapter nineteen

Lowell was the first one to jump up. "Are you nuts?" he yelled at Bruce. "Put that out!"

Bruce shrugged. "Can't. No water up here."

"You'll burn the whole barn down!" Juliet said.

"That's the idea, dogface."

The hay bale smoldered as they watched it, astonished by the turn of events. Suddenly flames shot up in back of Bruce. They were all on their feet by then, everyone but Patsy. She looked up at the burning hay, then turned around again and stared straight ahead. "I'm still going to win," she said quietly.

Bruce clambered down the ladder, and they all—all but Patsy—looked up at the hayloft in silence, as though they couldn't really believe what was happening. The few bales of hay that were left burned rapidly, and the flames jumped to the wooden walls and ceiling beams in seconds. The boards that had been tacked over the hayloft door went up fast, and a ray of sun burst through the hole, reminding them that there was a world outside the dark barn.

As the fire spread across the roof timbers and down one side of the building, smoke thickened and curled around them.

Annette banged on the door. "The barn's on fire! Mike! Juliet! Get out of there!"

Tommy was already coughing when he and Mike headed for the door. "Come on, everybody. Let's go. You can die just by inhaling smoke!"

"Come on, Patsy," Juliet said urgently, holding out her hand to her friend. "There's a well outside. Maybe we can figure out how to put the fire out."

"I don't want to put it out," Patsy said, not looking up. "You go ahead. I'm going to win this war."

Mike and Tommy pried the heavy door open and called back to the others to hurry up. "The ceiling's gonna fall in!" Mike yelled.

Lowell grabbed Juliet's arm. "Let's go!" he said.

"Patsy, come on!" Juliet said again.

"If Bruce is staying, I'm staying," Patsy said. "Besides, what difference does it make?"

Juliet knew exactly what she meant. "Don't think that way, Patsy! There might not even be a war! You don't know for sure!"

"Who cares?" Patsy said, closing her eyes. "Go outside, Juliet. Get out of here."

Juliet could feel the smoke clogging her lungs, and she

tried to cough it away. Lowell pulled her again, and she followed him to the door. What else could she do? Patsy wouldn't leave!

They stumbled out into the bright sunlight and away from the smoldering barn. When Juliet turned around to look back at it, she was astounded. The entire structure was burning now, flames leaping into the air and dancing down all four sides. There was no way they'd be able to put that out by themselves, even if they had buckets or a hose.

"Are Patsy and Bruce still in there?" Annette yelled.

Juliet nodded. "They won't leave. They both want to win."

"They're crazy!" Mike said. "This isn't worth dying for! I'm going for help."

"I'm coming with you!" Annette said, and they both started running up the road toward the farmhouse.

And then part of the roof fell in. The rumble and crash echoed inside Juliet's head, and she knew immediately it was a sound she'd never forget.

Within seconds Bruce emerged from the door, gray-faced and choking. He lurched away from the barn toward the well pump. "That girl is insane!" he yelled. "Nobody could stay in there!"

"She'll come out now that you did," Juliet said, but no other figure appeared in the dark doorway. Juliet walked closer. "Patsy!" she yelled into the fire. "You can come out now! You won!"

Bruce was gulping water from the well, but he stopped long enough to repeat himself. "She's crazy, I tell you!"

"You're the crazy one!" Tommy yelled back at him. "You set the barn on fire!"

"Yeah!" Lowell said. "And we're not taking the blame for it either. We're telling everybody that you did it!"

Juliet stared at the open barn door, knowing what had to be done but not sure she could do it. "We have to get her out! Maybe she's hurt or something! Maybe—" The sound of more falling debris cut her off.

"I'm going in," she said.

"Wait!" Lowell stripped off his sweatshirt and then the T-shirt underneath.

"What are you, Superman?" Bruce said, but the laugh caught in his throat.

Lowell took a penknife from his pocket and cut the T-shirt down the middle, then stuck both halves under the water pump. He wrung out both pieces of wet cloth and handed one to Juliet. "I read about this somewhere. We hold these over our mouths when we go in."

She nodded, the word "we" chiming in her head like a church bell. For the second time in the last few days a simple pronoun made her want to cry with relief. Instead she took Lowell's hand and they headed back into the barn side by side.

The smoke was so thick Juliet couldn't see her own feet.

"I can't see anything!" she said, her panicky voice muffled by the wet shirt. The heat of the fire made her feel like she was melting.

"Don't let go of me," Lowell said. "She was over here."

Juliet gripped Lowell's hand with one of hers and held the rag over her mouth with the other. She tried to take small, quick breaths, her heart beating double-time. It was clear to her that no one could survive in here for long.

"There she is! On the floor!" Lowell dragged Juliet closer until they were standing over Patsy, pulling at her arms.

"Patsy! Get up!" Juliet shouted at her. Patsy was lying on her back, eyes closed, mouth half open. She didn't move.

"Pick her up and run! Now!" Lowell ordered.

Juliet felt the burning air singe her throat, the fire steal her breath. She was so dizzy she wasn't even sure where the door was anymore.

Between bouts of coughing Lowell said, "I'll take shoulders—you take legs."

Somehow they managed to pick her up, but not without letting the cloths drop from over their mouths. Juliet's brain kept telling her she couldn't breathe, she couldn't lift Patsy, she couldn't do the impossible. But Lowell was pulling them toward the door, which was itself on fire now, and if he wasn't giving up, she wasn't either. There was a burning timber in their way, but they walked over it as if it were kindling wood. *Another few yards,* Juliet told herself. *Another few feet, another few inches.* As they finally dragged Patsy out into the sunshine, into the cool, clear air, Juliet heard the wonderful wail of the fire engines, coming at last, before she dropped to the ground and lost consciousness.

When Juliet awoke, she was in an ambulance with an oxygen mask strapped over her mouth. She turned her head and saw that Lowell was on the stretcher next to hers, also masked.

"What happened?" she said, but her voice was hoarse and muffled by the mask. She coughed again and lifted the corner of her mask so she could be heard. "Where's Patsy?"

Lowell looked over at her and lifted his mask too. "Another ambulance." His voice sounded as bad as hers.

"Is she okay?"

"I don't know," Lowell said. "I don't know."

The medic who was riding with them leaned over Juliet. "Glad to see you're back with us. Keep the mask on, okay? We'll be at the hospital in a few minutes."

"The other girl—Patsy—is she okay?" Juliet asked the young man.

He gave her a tight-lipped smile and positioned the mask back in place. "Don't know, honey; I was working on you. Don't worry—they'll take good care of her."

But that was no answer. No answer at all. Juliet closed her eyes and wished she could close her ears, too. The ambulance siren screamed in her brain, announcing to everyone who heard it, *Something is wrong. Something is very, very wrong.*

chapter twenty

"I don't understand how this could have gotten so out of hand," her mother kept repeating. "I thought it was just a game!"

"It was at first," Juliet croaked, her throat still sore. She'd coughed all night and slept very little, but finally this morning she'd felt a little better, and the nurse had taken the oxygen tubes out of her nose.

Don Klostermeyer paced up and down in front of the windows. "I gave you credit for more sense than this, Juliet," he said. "Didn't it occur to you that someone would get hurt playing these dangerous games?"

"Don't yell at her, Don," Ethel said.

"I'm not yelling. I'm trying to understand this."

Ethel sat with her head in her hands. "I should have been paying more attention when Patsy's mother told me the tests were dangerous. I should have put a stop to it. But no, I'm too busy stacking canned goods and counting up change."

"It's not your fault, Mom. It was hard to stop it once we

got started," Juliet said. "Nobody wanted to lose. Especially Bruce and Patsy."

"Well, they're the big losers now, aren't they?" her father said.

"Don!" Ethel scolded.

"I thought you said Patsy was going to be okay!" Juliet said, sitting up straighter in the bed. "You said—"

"She's much better," Ethel said, resting a reassuring hand on Juliet's arm. "But her burns are worse than yours and Lowell's, and the smoke inhalation damaged her lungs. I heard one of the doctors say she'll always have some trouble with her breathing. She won't be an athlete, that's for sure. But at least she's alive, thanks to you and Lowell. When I think of the two of you going into that burning building, I could cry. It was incredibly stupid, but it was also incredibly brave." And then Ethel did cry, the first time Juliet could recall ever seeing her mother in tears, including at her own father's funeral. *I guess it doesn't take polio,* she thought, *only smoke inhalation.*

This wasn't the first time in the last twenty-four hours that someone had called Juliet brave, and she found that it made her very uncomfortable. She hadn't felt brave going back into the barn—she'd felt scared to death. It was the last thing she'd wanted to do, but what choice did she have? She might even have given in to her fear if Lowell hadn't taken charge, handed her the wet cloth, and walked into that inferno by her side. She thought that maybe bravery was always at least part stupidity—or at least ignorance. But what if she hadn't gone back into the barn for Patsy? Nobody would be calling her a hero, that's for sure. They'd recognize her for what she really was: the same cowardly girl who hadn't wanted to sit in the barn in the first place, even when the only danger was skunks.

Caroline had been sitting quietly in a chair next to the bed, handing Juliet the glass of ice water with the bent straw whenever she asked for it. "Another minute inside the barn and Patsy wouldn't have made it," she said softly. "That's what the doctor told us. He said you and Lowell were heroes."

Don Klostermeyer exploded. "Yes, but heroes often die, Juliet. Think of that the next time you plan to do something this foolish!"

Juliet frowned. She hadn't planned to be a hero, and she didn't *want* to be one. She just wanted everything to be back the way it was before, when Patsy could run and skate and scream as loud as she wanted. When she and Lowell weren't hoarse and hurting. When the three of them didn't have painful burns on their legs and hands that would probably leave scars. Before the challenge had become a war.

Caroline brushed Juliet's hair gently out of her eyes. "It was all that Bruce Wagner's fault," she said. "And he didn't even get hurt. I bet he'll have to go to the juvenile detention center up in Belford. That's what he deserves."

Did he deserve that? Juliet wasn't sure. Of course, Bruce

was a wild, out-of-control kid. He was the one who'd kept pushing them to do things that were dangerous and dishonest. He'd lit the match and burned down the building, but it was just an old, empty barn. He hadn't thought anybody would get hurt. And he certainly hadn't known that Patsy needed to win so badly that she was willing to sit in there forever. It had never before occurred to Juliet how quickly one thing might lead to another: a prank, a bet, a challenge, a war.

At least nobody died in this war, she reminded herself. They were hurt, but they'd be okay, mostly. They'd never forget it, though—and they would never be exactly the same as they'd been before the fire.

"Oh!" Caroline said, rummaging in her purse. "I almost forgot. I bought you some comic books: *Archie* and *Betty and Veronica.* I know you'll probably be home by tomorrow, but I thought this would give you something fun to do today."

Juliet smiled at her sister. If she ever bothered to pray again, she'd definitely reinstate Caroline on the list of people she hoped to save. Although she was pretty sure she wouldn't bother anymore—it seemed like a useless exercise.

"Thanks." Juliet took the comics and began to page through them.

A nurse's aide came running into the room, her white shoes smacking the linoleum. "Turn on the television," she said. "Quick!"

Don was closest to the set, which was mounted on the

wall. Juliet felt suddenly sick to her stomach as he turned it on. This was it. The *real* war.

But the announcer had a smug grin on his face as he read the news. "I repeat," he said, "Soviet Premier Nikita Khrushchev has announced on Radio Moscow that he will remove all missiles from Cuban soil immediately. And so the crisis seems to be over. At least for now."

"Thank God!" Ethel said. "Kennedy did it!"

"I guess we showed them," Don said. "You can't push the United States around! We'll push right back!"

Caroline got weepy again, but she was laughing, too. "Did you hear that, Juliet? There isn't going to be a war!"

Juliet nodded. "At least for now," she said.

People in the hallway outside her room were yelling happily, "We won! We won!" Juliet felt relieved too, although she was almost afraid to get her hopes up that it was really over this time. *Besides*, she thought, *what had they won?* Everybody in the United States—and probably in Russia and Cuba too—had been terrified for a whole week. They'd thought constantly about death and destruction, about the end of the world. Now it wasn't going to happen—not this week, anyway. Still, you could never go back to the way you were before you knew it was possible.

The week Juliet returned to school, her mother announced to her daughters that she'd taken a part-time bookkeeping job four mornings a week for a lawyer in town. Mornings were usually not as busy in the store anyway, and they needed the money.

"I'll be much busier when I am here," Ethel told them, "so I expect the two of you to do more around the house now. You'll have to help with dinner in the evenings, and do some washing and ironing sometimes too."

Juliet waited for Caroline to complain about the unfairness of the situation; since she was the oldest, more would likely be expected of her. And for a moment she saw the flash of resentment in her sister's eyes, but it faded rapidly.

"I think it'll be fun to help with dinner. I want to learn to cook anyway," she said, a tight grin forcing up the corners of her lips. Which is when Juliet knew for certain that the past week had changed Caroline, too.

"Thank you, Caroline," Ethel said, and pulled both girls into an embrace. "Even though I'll be busy, I want you both to make me stop and listen to you when you need to talk to me. You're growing up, and I don't want to miss it!"

Juliet and Lowell were out of school for a week and Patsy for almost three. When Patsy did return, she was quieter. Not just her voice, which remained thin and hoarse from the tube the doctors had had to put down her throat, but everything about her. She didn't seem to want to talk much about the fire, so Juliet didn't bring it up either.

The small burns that Lowell and Juliet had gotten were almost healed, but Patsy still had a large bandage on her left hand, which made Juliet feel guilty. Her hand must have gotten burned when they were carrying her to the door; they hadn't been able to keep her arms from dragging along the floor. She knew how much it must hurt, especially when the bandage was changed. Juliet herself couldn't help crying when her mother smeared salve on the burns on her legs, and if her sister was in the room, Caroline cried a little too, just watching.

There had been some talk, at first, of having a public ceremony for Juliet and Lowell, at which they would receive medals for bravery. The mayor's office had talked to their parents, and their parents had talked to them. But neither Lowell nor Juliet was interested in having that kind of attention—and they didn't think Patsy would appreciate it either—so their parents explained to the city officials that the barn burning had been so frightening for them that they just wanted to forget about it. Which wasn't exactly true—they could never forget it anyway—but it was an explanation the officials understood. So instead of a ceremony, the mayor had some plaques made up and sent to them at home. Juliet hid hers in the back of her closet along with the newspaper article about the fire.

The problem with getting medals and recognition from people who thought you were brave was that they had the wrong idea of bravery. Juliet knew it only meant, *I have no choice.* There had been no moment when her brain said, *This is worth dying for.* Maybe her heart had said it, but she wasn't sure.

When she returned to school, Patsy was no longer able to ride her bike, but the weather was getting colder by then, so they probably wouldn't have ridden many more mornings anyway. Instead of Patsy's mom driving them, it was almost always her dad now. He'd gotten his hours changed at the base, Patsy told Juliet, so he'd be able to do it. "He wants to spend more time with me," Patsy said, a little embarrassed, but smiling.

For the first few days, when Patsy wasn't saying much, her dad kept up a constant chatter. "By spring we'll be riding bikes again, won't we, Patsy? I'm gonna get my old bike tuned up so I can ride too. We gotta get out and see what this country-side looks like around here. We're not in Arizona anymore!" He acted like he was a happy guy, but the minute he stopped talking, his eyebrows would sink down over his nose as if the effort of holding them in place were too much for him. He checked the rearview mirror every few seconds as if he thought Patsy might have disappeared since he'd last looked.

Patsy picked at the strings that unraveled from her bandage as though she were working out a difficult puzzle, but when they got to school, she leaned over the seat and gave her dad a kiss on the cheek.

Sometimes Lowell rode to school with them too. This,

Juliet thought, was the silver lining to the big ugly cloud of war—at least the war in Wisdom Hill. Without either of them having to say it, Juliet and Lowell had become best friends again. Actually, Juliet thought, they'd never really stopped being best friends; they'd only acted like they had. They both had other friends now too, and that was a good thing. Annette and Mike hung out all the time anyway, but none of the boys complained anymore if the girls came over when they were working on the go-kart—they all joked around together now. The boys even let Patsy help with the go-kart, since her dad was a mechanic and she knew about engines.

Still, Juliet knew that only your *best* best friend would go into a burning building with you. Lowell she would trust forever.

God she was less sure about, but since the worst had not happened, she thought it was possible somebody was paying attention after all. So she sent out one more prayer:

God, if you are real, or if you're Grandpa, or whoever you are, thank you for stopping the war, and for saving Patsy, and for giving me back my best friend, Lowell. If you didn't have anything to do with this stuff, you ought to know that everybody thinks you did, especially stopping the war and saving Patsy. I think Lowell and I figured out how to be friends again without any help. Anyway, I might talk to you again sometime or I might not. I know it sounds strange, but ever since the fire I'm not as scared of stuff like death anymore. I know now that I'll fight to live as long as I can, no matter how bad things get. Whether you're out there helping me or not.

Juliet thought that perhaps, if she decided to pray again, she might ask God about helping Bruce Wagner. Bruce had gone to the Belford Juvenile Detention Center, where he'd have to stay until at least Christmas and maybe longer. About a week after the fire Juliet and Patsy and Lowell all got letters from Bruce. They'd compared them and found them to be identical except for the headings.

"He just copied the same letter to all of us," Patsy complained. "He even misspelled the same words. I bet they made him write to us."

Juliet had been thinking the same thing, but when she went back and reread her letter, she felt a little more forgiving toward Bruce. Maybe they *had* made him write the letters, but at least he'd done it. And it couldn't have been easy.

To Juliet,
I'm sorry I set the fire I shouldn't have done it. I didn't think anybody would get hurt. I hope you feel OK now. My mom said she sees you waking down the alley sometimes so you must not have got hurt too bad. I promis to be nicer to you when I get out of here and come home. So don't be scared.
Bruce Wagner

Patsy was still grumbling about the letters as the whole group of them—boys and girls—walked to Linda's house after school one day.

"As if I'd ever be scared of *him*," she said.

"You're probably the only person who wasn't," Lowell said as they all followed Linda down the ladder into the bomb shelter. The boys wanted to see it, so Linda had planned the excursion for a day she knew her dad wouldn't be home until late and her mom would be too busy to notice.

"Don't shut the door!" Juliet reminded Lowell who was the last one down the ladder.

"Don't worry, I won't," he said. And she didn't worry.

They lined themselves up along the two lower bunks, and Patsy passed around a bag of brownies her mother had sent to school with her.

"I get anything I want now. It's boss," she said, which sounded almost like the old Patsy, the braggy one, except they all knew she wasn't the same, even if she tried to be.

It had been a month since the fire by then, but it was still on their minds all the time. Even with Patsy there it was too hard not to talk about it when they were all together. Annette couldn't hold back any longer.

"I've never been so scared in my life as when I saw that barn on fire," she said. "And then when Patsy didn't come out, I was sure I'd never see her again. Mike and I were running up the road to call the fire department when we heard them coming. I guess Mrs. Lutz saw the flames from her place—"

"When you guys came out, your faces were totally *gray*," Tommy said. "I never saw anybody look like that before."

"I wish I'd been there!" Linda said.

"No, you don't," Annette assured her. "Juliet passed out, and Patsy just looked . . ."

She stopped herself.

"Dead? Did I look dead?" Patsy asked.

Annette nodded.

Patsy grabbed another brownie from the bag and studied it intently. "I won, though, didn't I? Which means the challenge ended up four to four. A tie."

Juliet groaned. "You don't really care about that anymore, do you?"

Patsy didn't answer. She took a bite of the brownie and looked down at her bandaged hand.

"Nobody won," Lowell said. "And I'm glad nobody won. I hate fighting with people."

"It's cool that we're all friends now," Annette said. She grabbed Mike's arm. "I'm thirsty. Come up to the house with me to get drinks and glasses and stuff."

Tommy followed his brother up the ladder, because he was used to following him, and Linda followed Tommy, because Annette had signaled her to do so with her eyes.

Patsy stretched out on the lower bunk she had to herself now. Juliet and Lowell took off their shoes so they could sit cross-legged on the mattress across from her. Juliet was surprised at how comfortable she felt in the cozy little space now and leaned back against the wall.

Patsy was staring at the bunk above her, when suddenly she blurted out, "I'm sorry."

Juliet and Lowell said nothing; they didn't look at each other or move so much as a toe.

Patsy cleared her hoarse throat and continued. "I don't know why I didn't come out of the barn," she said. "I saw Bruce leave, and I heard you calling me, but it didn't feel like I'd won yet. I wanted to prove something to . . . somebody. I know it sounds dumb now. Then I guess I passed out."

"It's okay," Juliet said. What else could she say?

"I didn't mean for anybody else to get hurt." Patsy's eyes were suddenly damp, but she battled hard against tears.

"We know," Lowell said. "It's okay."

"It's not really okay," Patsy said. She sat up and turned her head to the side so she could wipe away the liquid without too much notice. "Anyway, thanks for coming in to get me. I'm sorry you got hurt." It was harder and harder for her to pretend she wasn't crying, and it really made her mad. "Darn it! I never cry!" she said, banging her foot on the floor. "Crying is for sissies."

"Like us, you mean?" Lowell said, laughing.

"Yeah," Juliet said. "We cry all the time! Boo-hoo!"

Patsy sniffed. "I guess that's why you two nosebleeds are best friends."

"I guess it's why we *three* nosebleeds are best friends," Juliet said.

Patsy grinned as she wiped her cheeks on her sleeves. "Really?"

Juliet nodded, and then nobody seemed to know what to say next. Fortunately, Lowell came up with something.

"What animal is half cockroach and half rabbit?"

"I don't know," Juliet said. "What animal?"

"Bugs Bunny!"

They all groaned, and Juliet elbowed him in the side, then said, "What's worse than finding a worm in your apple?"

"Finding half a worm!" Patsy yelled. "I've got one. What's gray and wears glass slippers?"

"Cinderelephant!" they all shouted together, then fell back across the bunks, laughing like crazy, forgetting for a moment that they had ever been fighting a war.

ellen wittlinger is the critically acclaimed author of *Gracie's Girl*, *Razzle*, and teen novels *Love & Lies*, *Parrotfish*, *Blind Faith*, *Heart on My Sleeve*, *Zigzag*, and *Hard Love* (an ALA Michael L. Printz Honor Book and a Lambda Literary Award winner). She has a bachelor's degree from Millikin University in Decatur, Illinois, and an MFA from the University of Iowa. A former children's librarian, she lives with her husband in Haydenville, Massachusetts.